THIS CHANGES EVERYTHING

DARA GIRARD

ISBN: 978-1949764420

THIS CHANGES EVERYTHING

Published by ILORI Press Books

ILORI PRESS BOOKS, LLC

P.O. Box 10332

Silver Spring, MD 20914

www.iloripressbooks.com

Table for Two

Gaining Interest

Careless Rapture

Dangerous Curves

Familiar Stranger

It Happened One Wedding

Unexpected Pleasure

Midnight Promise

Sweet Temptation

Always and Forever

Truly Yours

Say Yes

Clifton Sisters

The Sapphire Pendant

The Amber Stone

The Emerald Ring

Fortune Brothers

A Tempting Proposal

A Seductive Arrangement

An Unforgettable Moment

Novels

Honest Betrayal

The Daughters of Winston Barnett

Remember My Name

Illusive Flame

Winterwood Lane

Promise Me

CHAPTER 1

This changed everything.

Karen Palmer held back a gasp and bit her lip, feeling like the unwitting soon-to-be victim in a horror movie. She didn't like horror movies. She didn't like being scared, but the moment Joshua Akibu walked into the conference room she felt like screaming.

Her throat closed, her mouth felt dry, her heart started pounding. Not out of terror, although the large, black man with the dark eyes and trim goatee wasn't the friendliest looking chemical engineer she'd ever worked with. However, the sight of him wouldn't make her scream (although twice, with just a glance, he'd sent a shiver of fear through her) but she wasn't the only person he sometimes set on edge. She'd heard others whisper about him—sometimes about his brilliance but mostly about his aloofness and impatience. Behind his back they called him the Glacier, they probably also called him something less kind.

But Karen was used to working with difficult person-alities. Part of her thrived on it. *Give me your brilliance and I'll make it shine.* She hadn't worked to grow her company, 3R, a textile recycling development firm, by being a pushover. But today she felt something she hadn't felt in a long time. Some other equally awful feeling worse than terror. It slithered over her skin, turning her stomach into knots.

It was the feeling of dread. As if the cold grasp of a Delaware winter had seeped into the room chilling her flesh, tapping icy fingers across her neck until goose bumps danced along her arms.

She grabbed the glass of water in front of her and took a swallow, dribbling some on her chin. She quickly set the glass down, annoyed that her hand was shaking. She sent him a glance, relieved that he was moving a chair and hadn't seen her make a mess. She quickly wiped her chin and glanced down at her light red blouse where two wet spots had fallen and started to spread like ink stains.

She reached for the black jacket she'd hung on the back of the chair and quickly put it on. There, that was better. No one could see the water stains and by the time the meeting finished they should be dried. She took a deep breath, satisfied by her minor victory, then looked at Joshua again, which was a mistake because the sense of dread gripped her once more and she couldn't get her hands to stop shaking.

It wasn't supposed to happen like this. She was supposed to have a cool, civil professional chat with Joshua about his lack of growth and performance at the company. She'd chosen the small conference room as a neutral territory. It wasn't her favorite place, but served its purpose with its nondescript grey walls, a large oval brown table and seven plush grey seats. Her business partner, Marshall Holmes, had selected the furniture and told her they were top of the line (when she'd seen the bill she'd convinced herself he was right) and helped their business make a great impression on clients who visited their office.

Marshall felt a little uneasy about their location in Winchester, Delaware, a city in New Castle County that didn't have the history of Wilmington or the flash of other notable cities namely Newark. She didn't care that they weren't in New York or New Jersey. Delaware was the state of the Duponts and other smaller, although less notable companies, and the people they worked with didn't care about their location as long as 3R was able to supply them with the material they needed.

She knew how to make people trust her, she was also a mean negotiator and fair moderator. She'd come into this meeting remembering all that. She'd planned to gently let Joshua know he was being let go.

She felt her choice of words would be kinder than saying he was being fired. This meeting wasn't something she'd looked forward to. It had actually been something she'd been dreading for a week when Marshall told her that they no longer required his services.

After a quick scan of Joshua's performance review she had to agree. She'd been the one to hire him. It had been two years ago and she'd had hope for him, but nothing had come of it. She'd made it a policy that once someone had to part with the company she would do the deed. She didn't want to hide behind her position. She knew the name of each of the fifteen people who worked for them. She didn't want to become some impersonal corporate drone.

Today was the first time she wished she hadn't made that policy. That she could hide behind HR and not look back. But aside from a restless night, she'd been prepared. Marshall saw her as too accommodating. Today was the day she would prove him wrong.

Except she couldn't.

Because Joshua Akibu hadn't come alone.

He had a baby.

A cute little baby with a tiny birthmark on the temple, dressed in a bright green jacket. He held the baby in his right arm, while a large diaper bag draped his shoulder and two large black straps of his black backpack covered his chest.

"I'm really sorry about this," he said, dropping the diaper bag on the floor.

"Are you babysitting?"

"No."

Her brows shot up. "It's yours?"

He hesitated. "It's been a crazy morning, but I—"

"I understand," she said quickly, not quite knowing how to interpret the odd note in his voice. She couldn't tell if it was embarrassment (he didn't seem the sort who was easily embarrassed), frustration (he was an engineer, they loved being frustrated and solving problems) or annoyance. Whatever the reason, she didn't want the meeting to be any more awkward than it already was.

The feeling of dread slowly changed into something else. Something less frightening into something she could handle.

Understanding.

This baby explained everything. Now Joshua was no longer a mystery.

She now understood his tardiness, his tired face, his terse responses to others. He was a sleep deprived new father. Nobody would have ever suspected he had a life outside of work let alone a woman and a child. Yes, this changed everything. She couldn't fire him. Not now. Not three weeks before Christmas. A bachelor with no life was easy to let go, but a new father...

She would come up with a reason to keep him, he deserved a second chance. Marshall wouldn't like it but this man and his child were worth fighting for.

Karen reached for the glass of water again, this time with a steady hand. Her mind raced. She would tell Marshall that helping Joshua was the perfect opportunity to show how considerate they were to those employees with parental considerations. Good—no great—for their image. She took a long swallow and set the glass on the table. Yes, this would work.

Joshua sat. He didn't take off his backpack so he sat perched on the edge of the seat, placing the baby on his lap. "I can explain."

Karen shook her head, softening her words with a smile. "You don't have to. You're a dark horse, but I'm actually glad to find out."

He frowned. "Find out?"

"Why you've been the way you are. A number of

your colleagues have been complaining about your cold manner. But if I were sleep deprived I'd be the same."

His frown increased. "My cold man—"

She waved his words away. "Doesn't matter now. The truth is I was going to let you go, but now I'm going to fight for you. What's its name?" She motioned to the infant.

He hesitated. "You were going to fire me?"

Maybe she shouldn't have told him that, he looked more flustered than she'd expected him to be. No, not exactly flustered, shocked and a little annoyed. But she probably would have felt the same. She wouldn't focus on chit chat right now. "This isn't going to be easy, but with a second chance we can improve your performance. I wish you'd let us know your situation. We do allow telecommuting, there are ways you can work from home. We could have given you time off. We could have arranged for—"

"You were going to *fire* me?"

No, he didn't sound annoyed. He sounded angry, but she couldn't understand why he kept harping on that issue when it was no longer a problem. "Yes, but now—"

"May I ask why?"

"Why what?"

"Why you were going to fire me."

She cleared her throat. The sight of the baby in his arms should have softened his image, but somehow he appeared more fierce.

Joshua was not a classically handsome man. There was a beautiful magnificence to his angular West African features and dark lashes that were as long as a doll's, which would have been pretty on a woman as well as the full black eyebrows that looked drawn on with the perfection of a makeup artist.

But the lashes and eyebrows gave no softness to his features. There was nothing gentle about him. He wasn't incredibly tall, but carried himself in a manner as if he could soar above you. His dark eyes had a cutting glare that put anyone in his line of vision on alert. That's how he made her feel now. On edge. But she didn't want to feel that way. She was desperate to understand him.

Perhaps it was fear that colored his brown eyes to an almost iridescent black. Fear that he'd nearly lost the ability to provide for his family. He saw her as the enemy. She had to reassure him that his job was safe, at least for now. That she wanted to be, if not a friend, at least someone he could trust. "I told you that—"

"I'd like to know the specifics," he cut in. The sound of his cold, deep voice burned like a laser boring a hole through tissue paper, making her feel scorched. "I always do my best."

Karen sighed, the feeling of dread inching over her skin again. He didn't seem the type who would appreciate feedback, but she might as well address it. She opened her tablet and looked at his performance review. "According to the head of your division you're not a team player, you make the others feel inferior, you're brash, you're impatient, you've been late on more than one occasion."

"Except for the days I was late due to car trouble, those are generalities. I'm asking for specifics."

"Our form doesn't measure that."

"Perhaps it should."

This time she bristled. She didn't like his feedback about their form but, unfortunately, he was right. It was hard to fight against personal bias. What did 'not a team player' mean? All she saw was a number. Three out of ten. She could see him making people feel inferior, but was it on purpose or a misunderstanding?

The baby squirmed and made a soft cry. Joshua glanced at his watch.

"Is it feeding time?" Karen asked him, her edgy feeling growing. The last thing she wanted was a baby wailing on top of everything. "Do you need to warm up a bottle or something?"

"No." He searched through the diaper bag. Even when the baby started to cry (clearly he was taking too long to find what he was searching for) he looked resigned rather than angry. It was a stressful and tense time, but he was handling it well. But when the baby's cries intensified she wondered if the harried father had left the bottle at home and if they'd have to cut the meeting short so that he could get the baby something. She wondered if she'd have to drive him or... Finally, he pulled out a bottle, settled the baby down then started to feed it with a casualness that made it clear he'd done it many times before.

"What's the name?" Karen asked hoping to change the subject. The fierce look hadn't left his face and she desperately wanted it to. It was hard to have a civil conversation with someone who looked like they wanted to burn you alive. Joshua looked like the kind of man who could make the wind tremble with a glance or take down a giraffe with his bare hands.

"Did I have personal complaints?" he said, raising his voice above the baby's loud, sucking noises.

Karen held back another sigh. The man was stubborn. Why was he so hesitant to give her the baby's name? Was he being that petty? Didn't he realize she was on his side?

"Marshall said something, right?" Joshua continued.

She stood and took the seat beside him so there was no distance between them. "As I stated," she said, keeping her voice moderate and calm, "this is a misunderstanding that can be fixed."

"He said he'd try to get rid of me."

She'd never heard that. "When?" she asked surprised. She could never picture Marshall being so unprofessional.

"You didn't know that?"

"I'm sure it was a misunderstanding."

Joshua nodded. "If that makes you feel better," he said. His indulgent tone was offensive, as if he were speaking to a naive child who still believed in Santa Claus, but the tender way in which he held his child made her take hold of her temper. Joshua wasn't someone she had to like. That wasn't why she'd hired him. She'd felt he would be a great addition to their company and she still believed so.

"The point is you're not getting fired and we need to decide how to best work with your team."

He sent her a long look. "You like looking on the bright side of things, don't you?"

"Yes, why not?"

He sighed. "More reasons than you know."

She felt her patience thinning. He would teach his child the wrong life lessons by being so cynical. "Joshua, I really think that you're an amazing person. I believe that we can handle whatever has happened in a very simple way. What have you been working on recently?"

His brows shot up again. "You don't know?"

"Should I?"

"I sent you a full report of all my ideas awhile back, some that even my colleagues had agreed on. I also listed possible concerns that need to be addressed over the next six months."

She hated being caught by surprise, even worse, not knowing what was going on in her own company. How could his performance review say that he was disruptive, uncooperative and lacked initiative when he'd just told her of a report that showed the direct opposite? And his colleagues had agreed with him? Something was going on.

"Are you sure you handed it in?" she said. "As a new father—"

"Of course I'm sure. Ask Marshall. I gave him a hard-copy to discuss with you."

Careful Karen. She took a deep breath. She didn't want to put him on the defensive. Otherwise her little boat of goodwill would be wrecked by an iceberg. She smiled. "It's probably lost somewhere on my desk."

"I sent a softcopy too."

"And my computer," she quickly added, "and I haven't gotten to it. It's my fault and I apologize."

"Why would you apologize for something you aren't sure about yet? What if you never received it?"

"I'm sure that's not the case. Anyway, I will look over your report and get back to you as soon as I can." She lightly touched his hand. "In the meantime, if there is anything you need let me know."

Joshua stood and slung the diaper bag over his shoulder. "I'm fine, thanks." He walked to the door.

Karen wouldn't have thought much of his cool dismissal if she hadn't spotted two pretty baby brown eyes, gazing at her over his broad shoulder, making her smile.

CHAPTER 2

"*A* baby?"

For the second time that day Karen felt her heart pounding at the sight of a man. But this time it was for very different reasons. Her business partner, Marshall Holmes, never terrified her, although she didn't look forward to the news she'd have to tell him: That she hadn't fired Joshua. She knew that would upset him, but that wasn't what made her heart race.

It was his beauty.

He was a beautiful man to look at. Today he'd covered his exquisitely proportioned body in dark trousers and a baby blue shirt that seemed to make his brown skin glow and he sat behind his glass desk looking as if he were a model for an international fashion magazine or an online influencer with millions of followers. She could imagine following him—taking note of his every movement. For nearly ten years she basically had— aware of every holiday trip he'd taken, car he'd bought, girlfriend he'd dated—and most times he didn't know she was alive.

Well, no, he knew she was alive, but he didn't see her as anything, except his business partner. Most times she felt, instead of seeing a woman, he saw her as a large spreadsheet and profit and loss chart. That was when she didn't feel like he was looking right through her. Not because he was cruel. He was far from that, but because his mind was always focused on the business. He only saw her as an extension of that.

That probably wouldn't have bothered her so much if she wasn't in love with him.

She'd been in love with him for years. Not only because he was model handsome, but because he was genuine, kind, and smart. 3R, which stood for Recycle, Reuse, Reinvent, wouldn't have existed without him. He'd helped to make her dream come true, which always made it difficult to go against him.

But this time was different.

"Akibu has a baby?" Marshall repeated when Karen didn't speak.

"Yes, I know. It's amazing. I couldn't imagine him with a pet, let alone a girlfriend or wife. And to be a father?" She briefly covered her mouth as another thought struck her, "What if he's a single father and—"

"So what?"

Karen paused. "I'm sorry?"

"So what? How does this change anything?"

Karen shifted in her seat. Perhaps she hadn't been clear when she'd explained the situation. "I can't fire him—"

"Of course you can. We're not running a charity here. People need to pull their weight."

"He does that. I looked at his performance review and it didn't really give me specifics about—"

"It's specific enough, his marks are low."

"And he told me about the report he submitted with ideas that—"

"He's toxic."

Karen opened her tablet confused. "I didn't see that written anywhere."

Marshall waved his hand. "It doesn't have to be written down to be true. His colleagues don't like working with him."

"Perhaps if I spoke to them—"

"They spoke to me in private on different occasions. I said that I would handle this for them. Do you want to make me look like a liar?"

"No," Karen said surprised that all of Joshua's colleagues would have spoken to Marshall first instead of her. She'd thought she'd made them feel that they could come to her with any concerns. However, she didn't want to make Marshall feel bad if they'd confided in him. She'd have to accept that. She clasped her hands in her lap. "I would like to find a better way to handle this than to cut him out without—"

"You're too soft. You were swayed by theatrics."

"Theatrics?"

"Yeah," Marshall said warming to his subject. "What if the baby was a prop? A last ditch effort to keep his job?"

"That's ridiculous."

"What's even more ridiculous is you falling for it."

"I'm not falling for anything," she said hurt by his criticism. But this had been a sore point between them for years. He didn't like her hands-on approach with the employees. He wanted her to present a more hard-line edge, but she didn't feel she needed to be a ball-buster to be successful and she certainly wasn't going to fire a new father so close to the holidays. She folded her arms, her conviction making her feel strong. "Actually, what happened today with Joshua brings me back to how we conduct performance reviews. I thin—"

Marshall rolled his eyes. "Not this again."

"Yes, this again. It's important. I don't think the number system for evaluating people works well."

"It works for my father's company and many others. It works for us too."

Karen didn't think so but didn't want to argue right now. That would come later. "Joshua deserves a second chance."

"Fine he's got a month. He either improves or he's gone and you too."

She blinked. "What?"

"You heard me. If he doesn't improve, you'll let me buy you out."

CHAPTER 3

Karen felt like she'd been slapped. Marshall had toyed with the idea of buying her out in the past, especially when she offered up ideas that would take the company in a direction he wasn't willing to go, and the money he had offered had been impressive. But she loved 3R, it was her heart and she didn't want to give it up. Or him.

Marshall grinned like a naughty boy offering a dare he knew she wouldn't take. "Are you still willing to risk it?"

"They are two totally different agendas."

"No, it's one. We're in a growth mode and we need to be on the same side. If you want to contradict me this way it will cause trouble in the future. Better we stop now rather than later. So agreed?" He leaned forward and softened his voice. "You can say no."

Her mouth felt dry again. He wasn't joking. He really wanted her gone. Her heart cracked. He truly didn't care about her. He was making it clear that he didn't see her as anything else but something that blocked him on his path to greatness. He was letting her know that he could run 3R alone.

He didn't need her. It was that realization that stung. She'd lost her usefulness.

She swallowed hard. She wouldn't let that be. She would prove that she was important to the company and especially to him. She would show him what she was made of. She would take him back to that night in the university library when they'd both been graduate students. He'd shown her his ideas for his capstone proposal and despaired of making sense of it and she'd helped him put it together.

She remembered when he'd called her up and told her about the professor's enthusiasm. She'd congratulated him and encouraged him to implement the project in the real world. He'd agreed and asked her to join him. Without hesitation she'd said yes. Although the following years had been difficult, they'd finally gotten the company to where it was now successful and they had a lucrative partnership. She wouldn't let him or the company go.

Marshall folded his arms and leaned back as if sensing her hesitation. "If you want me to talk to Akibu, I'll be glad to."

He was giving her an out. That was the Marshall she knew. The considerate man. The one who looked out for others. He was only trying to make her realize how important it was that they had the same vision; that they worked as a team. He didn't really want her to go against him. He wanted to feel that he could trust her. She needed to prove to him that he could.

She looked at his eyes. His chocolate brown gaze drew her in, almost pleading with her to agree. To let him take over and get rid of Joshua for both their sakes.

Why would she risk what they had for a surly engineer with fierce dark eyes?

But then the image of a baby's jacket and diaper bag thrown over a broad shoulder, already weighed down by a large backpack, flitted through her mind. Joshua deserved a second chance. She felt it in her gut. She knew he was good for the company, she'd sensed it the first time she'd recruited him. She was eager to see what kind of ideas he had. The thought gave her a different kind of excitement she hadn't had in years. She straightened in her seat and cleared her throat. "There's no need," she said.

"You'll fire him yourself?"

"No, I want to keep him and see some of his ideas."

"They're an expensive waste of time. Everyone says so."

"Everyone isn't me." She paused. "Wait...you read his report and didn't tell me?"

He cleared his throat. "I thought you had better things to do. You're a busy woman. You'd just returned from an out of town trip—"

"You should have let me be the judge of that."

He shrugged. "It's no different now. You'll be wasting your time."

"I don't think so."

Marshall looked at her surprised. "You'd really take the risk?"

"Yes, really. I'll look for a project or idea that will show you his worth. If he fails I fail, but if he doesn't, he gets a promotion."

"And what do you get?"

A chance to prove that you can trust me, that I'm the woman for you. I'll make you realize you need me and love me. "You have to implement whatever we come up with, without any argument and give me a bonus." To her delight he hesitated. "Unless you want to forget this stupid idea and—"

Marshall shook his head and surged to his feet. "I'm sorry I said anything. I don't want to lose you."

Karen stared up at him in wonder. "Really?" Did this mean he cared? Had the thought of losing her helped him see how valuable she was?

"Of course not. I've gotten use to you." He rubbed the back of his neck. "It would be stupid to lose you because you don't know how to read people."

She felt her hopes slowly fade.

"I don't want you putting something so important on the line for a guy like him." Marshall came from behind his desk and stood in front of her. "I know you feel a kinship because you scouted and hired him, but these are important times. It's not like you to be rash."

She surged to her feet so that he didn't tower over her. While she didn't meet him eye to eye, at least she'd close some of the distance. "I'm not being rash."

"You think you can take one of his ideas and make it work within a month?"

"No, I expect to prove to you the feasibility of what one of his ideas can do for the company within a month. Naturally we'll need more time to implement it. But by January you'll see his worth and improvement."

Marshall tilted his head, a slight smile on his lips. He glanced down at her tightly gripped hands. "You're nervous."

"I know."

"And you still want to do this?"

"Yes."

He rested his hands on his hips. "Maybe I don't know you as well as I thought I did."

Karen grinned, her heart beating fast. He was already seeing her in a new way. That was good. It was a starting point. "Maybe it's time I showed you."

She almost didn't make it into the hallway. Her legs shook so badly that she feared they'd crumple beneath her as she walked out of Marshall's office into the blue carpeted tunnel that served as a corridor.

Their building had formerly been a radio station with lots of different rooms. Karen didn't particularly like it. The white building reminded her of something built by an angry seven year old. Most of the rooms didn't have windows; the halls were so narrow she always held her breath every time she had to pass someone coming from another direction, lest she take up too much room. Each room could only fit two desks so it didn't make for an easy flow of ideas even when everyone kept their doors open.

However, she was able to get the break room expanded enough for more than four people to sit and converse. She'd wanted a more home office like atmosphere, but Marshall liked the idea of having a two storied building with history. Her one consolation was that a fun café was within walking distance on the other side of a park only a few blocks away. Plus, Marshall's father had helped him buy the building and restructure it a little.

But not enough to let Karen hide as she made her way down the blue hallway. She nodded her head at a staff member walking past.

She held onto the wall as she quickly made her way to her windowless office. Once there, she closed the door and collapsed into a chair. She couldn't believe what she'd just done. She'd spoken up to Marshall. She'd challenged him. She'd never done that before.

She half wanted to run back into Marshall's office and tell him she was sorry. That she was wrong. That they could come to another compromise. She wanted him to like her. What if she failed? What if she disappointed him or worse truly proved that he didn't need her anymore? She didn't want him to think of her as a habit he'd gotten used to. She wanted him to see her as a woman he couldn't live without.

That day in the university library, when she'd turned his hodgepodge of ideas into a working plan, she'd only wanted to get into his good graces. He'd already made a reputation for himself at the university. He was a debate team champion. She knew he had the mind, she knew logistics, and before they realized a simple idea for a college project had turned into a lucrative business.

It hadn't hurt that Marshall's father had also mentored them since he ran a successful construction equipment manufacturing company. His father was a very gracious man who took pride in his son's achievement. Still did. Every once in a while he'd travel from his Pennsylvania home, where he'd moved a couple years ago, to see how they were doing. He was a charismatic man with a sharp mind.

But she'd now started to dread his visits a little. Although, they ran a tight ship, Mr. Holmes thought there was room for larger profits. While that was true, she hadn't gotten into the business just for the money, but to make a difference. To stem the tide of waste that occurred in the fashion industry. 3R was only one tiny solution. The company took old clothing and used a solvent they had developed, to turn cotton and other fabrics into a pulp to create a new material for use in making clothing. They sold the material to ten key clients. One was a clothing and outdoor garment maker with a national chain of stores and a commitment of doing what's best for the environment for the long term instead of focusing on short term profits; another provided a line of uniquely dyed material to designers in the fashion industry.

But every year, when Mr. Holmes mentioned making more money, Marshall wanted to increase investment in marketing and promotion, while she wanted to stay small and nimble enough to keep ahead of changes and stay true to their vision of creating fabulous clothes without harming the planet and being a company their clients could rely on. A company with a vision.

She had wanted to be a textile designer until she

learned about the level of fabric related pollution in the clothing industry. Before meeting Marshall, she'd thought she'd make new creations from vintage clothing and teach people how to come up with new designs on their own without buying something new every couple of months. She even considered working with online influencers and style leaders to make re-wear, wearing an outfit more than once, fashionable again instead of something your grandparents did.

But Marshall's idea allowed her to think bigger, to reach farther than she'd ever dreamed. However, the last several years she'd felt stuck. Business was okay, they were profitable and making a difference, but the passion was lost.

Somehow the sight of a bright green jacket and a pair of wide brown eyes had reignited that passion. That baby represented the future.

A future she had to fight for now.

It was the reason she'd been prepared to take Marshall's disapproval.

Karen sat back, her legs no longer feeling weak. Standing up to him had sort of felt good. Was it the holiday season? The time of good cheer? Or the way Joshua had looked at her dumbfounded as he held his baby in his arms?

That image would never leave her.

Her mother had had the same expression when Karen's father had told her he was leaving. She'd never suspected anything was wrong. He didn't leave her for another woman, just said that he wanted a different life.

He said the words in a calm manner as he carefully

scooped up his red beans and rice before placing his knife and fork on the dining table. She remembered the sound of his chair scraping against the wooden floor as he stood to leave. She turned to her mother who sat frozen, mumbling the words, "A different life, a different life" over and over again. It had taken a huge pot of tea—"PG Tips, dear not Tetley"—to get her mother to calm down.

Karen still wondered why she hadn't raced after her father, shouting her shock and fear. Why she'd calmly put the kettle on as she heard his footsteps walk to the front door. Why she hadn't tried to stop him as he carried two suitcases he'd packed and placed them in the trunk of his silver Acura (silver like a rocket, he used to tease her. A decal of the NASA symbol still in the same place where she'd stuck it as a ten year old). She didn't know why she hadn't run to the window as she heard the soft roar of his engine before he backed out of the driveway and, like a rocket, disappeared from their lives.

She still wondered why her mother hadn't been angry with him. Why she had sipped the hot tea, without cooling it as if the steaming liquid didn't burn, with tears streaming down her face, but never let a harsh word leave her lips.

At sixteen, Karen didn't know how to comfort her mother, how to deal with a rejection that she felt as keenly as her mother did. She couldn't make sense of his words. Why did he want a different life? What did he mean by that? Weren't they good enough? Couldn't he come back? What had she done wrong?

It was only later that evening, alone in her room where she stared at a poster that glittered like a galaxy when the lights were off, that she wondered why he hadn't given them a chance to convince him to stay. Or why she hadn't tried to seize it herself.

She felt that she'd somehow failed them both.

Her guilt didn't subside when he returned to them a year later. She remembered letting him hug her, feeling as if she were in the arms of a stranger even though he smelled the same, like liquid pens and ginger. He told them he missed them.

Karen had a litany of questions—Where have you been? Kingston? Port Antonio?—but one look from her mother forced her to bury them deep in her heart, where they caused a sharp pain, like a splinter under the skin.

Her mother eagerly welcomed her father back, reminding Karen in urgent whispers not to bother him with silly questions, just in case anything they said or did made him leave again.

But she never trusted him after that. Never felt comfortable at dinnertime, too aware of all the words not spoken, too aware of the year when his chair sat empty.

Two months after his return, on Thanksgiving Day, among the scent of cranberry sauce and warm cornbread, he told them he'd come back because he'd missed them (yes, she'd heard that before) and realized there was no other home out there for him. That he treasured them more than he ever knew.

His words made her mother happy, but his explanation never satisfied Karen. Never helped to remove the hurt and the shock he'd put her mother through. And that look on her mother's face still haunted her. That look of loss and devastation.

Briefly, Joshua had something similar in his gaze. She saw past the brilliant posturing to a man with something to lose. She could tell that this job meant more to him than they'd suspected and she would allow him the chance, a chance her father had never given her, to prove himself, even if that meant annoying Marshall.

Especially if that meant annoying Marshall.

One day Marshall would beg her to stay.

He'd already started to see her in a new light and she'd use that to her advantage.

CHAPTER 4

Marshall closed his eyes, hung his head and softly swore.

Akibu was staying.

That egotistical bastard Joshua Akibu was staying. What had he done wrong?

It had all been perfectly planned. Getting rid of him should have been easy. It would have been easy if...

How could he have a kid? And why would Karen fall for that? She usually did what he told her, that's how it worked. That's how it *always* worked.

He knew—hell everyone knew—she had a queen size crush on him. And he didn't see anything wrong with that. It made her easy to work with and he liked working with her. She was always eager to please and did what he told her. She made him look good. Who wouldn't want someone like that by their side?

She only had one tiny thing to do today and she'd

defied him. He didn't like being defied and what bothered him more was that it wasn't the first time.

The first time happened two years ago when he'd come back from a holiday trip to Spain and Portugal and discovered she'd hired Akibu without telling him.

She shouldn't have done that. Okay, so a week long holiday had turned into four. That hadn't been his fault, part of it was research. She knew that. She should have understood. He had told her he was researching what other likeminded companies were doing and seeing what new partnerships he could make.

They'd both agreed that they'd consult each other before accepting new hires so that they could keep the culture of their company under control. They—or rather she—didn't want to grow to the level where people became nameless and faceless bots. She didn't want to hire too many people and later be forced to fire them because of budget issues.

A new hire was a risk.

A new hire had to be carefully considered by the both of them.

But she'd broken that rule because she said Akibu was astonishing. Those were her exact words. Not amazing. Not incredible. *Astonishing*. Her description still put his teeth on edge. She'd never spoken about anyone else like that before or since.

"His reputation precedes him," she'd told him over the phone as he straightened his tie in his hotel room. He was preparing for a date with a woman who wanted to improve her English. He hoped they wouldn't be doing much talking at all. He had been annoyed by Karen's call and eager to leave, but news that she'd hired someone in his absence had caught his attention. "I'd heard rumors that he was unhappy where he was working and contacted him and expressed my interest."

"It's not like you to poach other people's talent."

"I didn't poach," she gently corrected him. "I approached him and really didn't think he was listening to anything I was saying."

Marshall pulled on his jacket that the cleaning service had just finished ironing. "You're not making any sense."

"I'd read one of his papers so when I told him at the conference—"

"Conference? What conference?"

"The one in New York. The one you decided not to go to."

There were many of those. He didn't really like discussing their industry with others. He had no idea there were so many fabric and textile conventions both in the US and abroad. Plus, there were additional small shows that helped new designers connect to distribution channels and companies like theirs. The last conference he'd attended had been several years ago in the UK. He'd fumbled his way through. It made him feel inadequate while Karen seemed to thrive in such places, so he always felt good sending her to them. This time he regretted his decision.

"And so I hired him," he heard her say. It was only then he realized that she'd continued speaking. He didn't want her to repeat her story so he only made a noncommittal sound. He told himself things would be fine. That it didn't matter that she'd done something so impulsive until he met Akibu.

It was a week after he'd spoken to Karen, when he was walking through the office corridor and spotted one of their engineers, a woman with thin brows and a name he didn't care to remember, talking to a man in his late twenties/early thirties that he hadn't seen there before. The corridor was too narrow for him to walk past with only a nod; one of the two would have to step aside to let him pass, which the man did.

And Marshall noticed he looked oddly familiar.

Very familiar.

Too familiar.

For a moment he thought he'd be sick. It had been nearly twenty years but the guy looked the same. Only bigger, no longer a kid. The engineer smiled when she saw him and said, "I didn't realize you were back. I was just showing him around."

"Don't let me stop you."

The man held out his hand. "Joshua Akibu."

The face may have changed a little but he definitely knew that name.

Marshall didn't move for a moment remembering that this was supposed to be the first time they'd met. Of course it was! They were strangers. The man didn't recognize him. Didn't make the connection. It was too long ago and brief. He was safe. He smiled and shook his hand. "Glad to have you on the team."

Akibu's grip was solid and sure. He had a capable grip. It was a grip that made Marshall nervous. Marshall left the two people in the hall and returned to his office wondering if he'd missed any clues. Did Akibu really not remember him or was it just a ploy?

Two years later Marshall still wasn't sure, although Akibu hadn't done anything to indicate that he knew Marshall or knew what he'd done. That didn't matter. He wouldn't have thought much more about it if Akibu hadn't been so good at his job.

He exceeded it. He was—he hated to admit it —astonishing.

The truth was Marshall wanted to get rid of Akibu because he was dangerous. Not because of what he might know about Marhsall's past but because of the present.

Akibu was after his job. That African bastard could run everything single-handed. Karen didn't see that. But she could be blind, unlike him. He could read people and Akibu was a man with ambition and too many ideas.

Within six months of joining the company Akibu had actually organized a think tank session with five other employees, forcing Marshall to quietly find a way to dismantle it. That kind of initiative had to be stopped. His father had shown him how dangerous it was when workers had too much autonomy. They started asking questions, expressing their concerns, which lead to disruption. He called Akibu into his office and gave him a warning that his renegade ways weren't welcomed there.

Marshall liked things as they were. Their business model worked and he didn't want to change it. They could make more money by growing their marketing arm and expanding what they were good at. Innovation was for others. 3R was too new to make some of the changes

Akibu suggested and also, too established to leave the well beaten path to bigger profits.

Yes, Akibu needed to go, but he didn't want to lose Karen too.

Karen.

Akibu had forced him to lie to her. He'd manufactured the poor performance review. Nobody had filed any complaints against Akibu, which bothered him even more. No matter how much he tried to dig, how much he tried to suggest otherwise, people stayed loyal. Everyone said that Akibu had some eccentric ways, but that they didn't find him offensive. He was a great worker; a solid, dependable colleague. He was called the Glacier because he could freeze you with a glance, but nothing more sinister behind the nickname.

Everyone liked Akibu.

Except him. And now he realized how dangerous this interloper truly was. Twice he'd managed to get Karen to act out of character.

Marshall was used to being the only person able to influence her. But something about Akibu made her act different. Perhaps he was trying to undercut him. Perhaps that was part of his plan to try to take his place.

He wouldn't let that happen. But he had to be clever.

Marshall opened his eyes and lifted his head. He still couldn't believe the bastard had a kid.

And it must have been one cute baby to melt Karen's heart like that. He knew it hadn't been easy for her to stand up to him. But she was standing up for a guy and his baby.

Marshall swore again, wondering the best way to outmaneuver that scenario.

The business needed Karen too much; more than she knew. Not that he'd ever tell her. That would make him weak and his father had shown him that weak people get beaten.

He had to win this battle. He'd been reckless in placing their little wager, but he'd see that Akibu failed, give Karen a chance to reconsider her choices then return everything back to the way it needed to be.

The way it had to be.

CHAPTER 5

*H*e had the DART system to blame for this.

If he hadn't taken the bus, none of this would have happened.

Joshua rolled up the soiled diaper and tossed it in the trash bin that stood next to where he was kneeling on the floor. He knew he couldn't leave it there long before it started to smell. Luckily, his co-worker was out for the day, so he had the office to himself. He grabbed a wet wipe and cleaned the baby up before he took out a fresh diaper and sighed. Yes, the Delaware Public Transportation system was to blame for all this.

Less than five hours ago he and this baby had been complete strangers. Still were if he was being completely honest. He'd only just discovered what sex she was because of the diaper change, which was why he couldn't offer Karen a name when she kept asking him for one.

Joshua briefly closed his eyes and sighed. If he'd hired a taxi or a car, because his ten year old Toyota was in the shop, he wouldn't be in this mess. But he'd also be without a job too.

He still couldn't believe he was about to get fired.

Fourteen pounds of cuteness had just saved his job. He would have laughed if he wasn't so annoyed.

If he hadn't taken the bus, he wouldn't have noticed the fresh faced young black woman with short black hair and a dangling gold earring in one ear. She also wore a large brown scarf that covered the lower half of her face, only showing her eyes.

The bus stop was so crowded he had to stand outside the shelter and stare at the large poster for the latest superhero movie. It was a chilly day, cold enough to let them know that 'winter' was just a name of a season that would come when it damn well wanted to.

They hadn't been hit with the blistery snow and ice pounding the northern states; they had the mountainous regions of Pennsylvania to thank for that. The mountains blocked the cold northeastern winds from hitting Delaware as hard as they could.

Instead of white skies and below freezing temperatures, not to mention snow, the clear, crisp day made him regret wearing his grey wool coat, black gloves, knit cap and green scarf. He looked like a man ready for a snowstorm, but he'd overdressed because he hadn't taken public transportation in a while and didn't know how long he'd be standing outside.

He kept the cap on but decided to remove his gloves before he pulled out his cell phone. He'd been looking at a message, which let him know his car would be ready by tomorrow, when someone bumped into him.

He looked up and saw the young woman's startled expression before she quickly readjusted her scarf to cover her face again. He absently brushed aside her apology, before he noticed she'd dropped a funny looking bobble head toy of a fairy on the ground and he handed it back to her. She enthusiastically thanked him as if he'd found her wallet or something, making him briefly wonder if women in their late teens or early twenties were always so exuberant. He brushed her enthusiasm aside as well before he glanced at other messages on his phone then put it away.

A bus came and most of the people got on, leaving the shelter and bench clear. Joshua unwrapped his scarf and took a seat, then stuffed the scarf in his backpack.

He should have suspected something was wrong when the young woman placed the baby on the bench beside him.

"Just for a second?" she asked, her voice and eyes pleading, "I have to quickly talk to someone," and he said, "Sure," and watched the young woman rush over to a car missing a hubcap on the back tire. He'd put his backpack back on when he noticed the baby rolling towards the edge of the seat. Fearing for its safety he jumped up and grabbed it.

Had that been a mistake? Maybe.

Maybe it wasn't going to fall.

Maybe if he'd let it fall and it had cried the mother would have rushed back instead of getting into an old black Lincoln and driving away.

He still couldn't believe when he saw her in the passenger seat leaving.

She. Was. Leaving.

Leaving!

He was too stunned to do anything but stand there and stare. Part of him thought she'd stop the car and let him know she'd gotten a ride. If he hadn't been so stunned he would have gotten a license plate number or something.

But he didn't. He just stood there.

Finally waking from his paralysis he spun to the two other people there. "Wait, did you just see that?"

"See what?" an older gentleman, wearing a tweed overcoat, said.

Joshua nodded to the now nonexistent black Lincoln. It must have turned down a side street. "That woman just left her baby."

"What woman?"

The teenager in pink combat-style boots shrugged. "I didn't see anything."

Joshua motioned to the bench. "She put her baby down right *here* and told me to watch it and then just left."

The teenager shrugged again. "Whatever you say."

Joshua shifted his gaze to the other man who shrugged as well. If only this had happened before the first bus had arrived. There would have been more witnesses. He glanced down, surprised by how calm the baby was when he felt as if his heart would leap out of his chest.

He heard the air breaks hiss for the next bus stopping in front of them like a great metal beast. He grabbed the diaper bag, hurried up the stairs, paid his fare and said to the driver, "I need you to contact your superiors—"

The skinny woman with a perm glared at him. "You've got a complaint? I arrived on time and—"

"No, it's not that."

"You need to take a seat, sir."

"But this woman—"

"Sir, you're holding everybody up. Please take a seat."

Joshua softly swore.

"What did you say?"

He briefly shut his eyes, wishing he hadn't said it so loud. "Nothing. The baby sneezed," he said then made his way down the aisle. The bus driver wouldn't be any help and no one had seen the woman.

He had no other choice.

That's what he told himself when the bus finally arrived at the stop near his office. He gently placed the baby on the backseat, set the diaper bag down then hurried off the bus.

Now it was someone else's problem. They'd go down the aisle, do a check of the seats and find it and everything would be fine.

He was only a few yards away when he heard the hush of the bus wheels halt and the doors open. The booming voice of the bus driver said, "Sir, sir!"

He started walking faster.

"Sir, your baby!" He turned around and saw an older brown skinned woman in a fashionable black coat holding the baby out to him. "You should never be in such a hurry you forget what's important to you," she said in reproach, but softened her words with a smile.

Joshua shook his head as he took the diaper bag and infant. "But it's not—"

The woman turned and got back on the bus and he watched the doors close. He sighed and looked down at the infant. It blinked up at him. He half expected it to burst into tears, he could take tears. He felt like crying too.

But the baby didn't cry. Its blinkless stare seemed to follow his face with intense curiosity. It looked to be about six months old and by this age would be wary of strangers. But the baby was looking around as if nothing was wrong.

"Has your mother done this before?" He could just imagine her making a tearful plea to the public, telling them of some man who'd stolen her baby. When he returned the child, would he be charged with kidnapping? Would she try to get money out of him? Or perhaps she'd just been desperate and didn't know what to do with an infant. But why a bus stop and why choose him?

Of all the people there, why had he been the sucker? She could have dropped this baby off anywhere. Why at a bus stop?!

As office workers, delivery drivers, and school kids hurried past him he'd never felt so alone. Like an island in the middle of an ocean. He knew he looked ridiculous but nobody seemed to notice. He felt both visible and invisible at the same time. But he couldn't think of that now.

He had no choice but to take the baby with him. He was already running late and today he had an important meeting with one of the company owners that could be good or bad. He hurried into the building ignoring the looks sent him as he made his way to the meeting. After the meeting was over, he'd call the police and tell them his story and then that would be that.

When he entered the conference room and saw Karen's face he almost started to laugh.

She looked so horrified and dismayed to see him with a baby he was eager to quickly assure her that he'd handle this situation. He was prepared for whatever question she leveled at him. She was one of the most easily readable people he'd ever met. He was surprised she'd managed to stay in the cutthroat business world as long as she had. There was nothing cruel and cutthroat about her. People genuinely liked her. He probably would like her too if he bothered or cared enough, but he didn't. People got in his way and he didn't have much use for them. People were too unpredictable.

Today had shown him how much.

He'd never expected that the fresh faced Karen Palmer of the tailored designer suits accented with floral scarves, smooth brown skin, pretty mouth, sparkling eyes and slicked back hair had wanted to talk to him so that she could fire him.

Fire *him*.

He still couldn't believe it. He should have. 3R wouldn't be the first job he'd been let go from, the previous time had been due to a merger, not because of his performance. He'd thought he'd found his place here. She'd been the one to convince him to come and now...

Fire him?

He prided himself on doing a good job. He'd given his

all to every project. He was cordial to his colleagues; he didn't go out with them after hours, but he'd thought they'd gotten used to him by now.

Okay, so he hadn't shaved in a couple days and his clothes were wrinkled, but didn't his ideas mean more than that? He worked best at night. And he'd been late by five minutes due to car trouble.

What more did they want?

Or was it Marshall? He didn't know why the guy was out to get him. He hadn't seemed to like him since the first day they'd met in the hallway. He still couldn't forget how cold and sweaty the other man's hand had been. But Joshua didn't care about being liked as long as he did a good job. So Marshall hated his think tank sessions, Joshua realized his mistake was that he hadn't invited him, the man probably felt slighted. And Marshall didn't like some of his office improvements, perhaps he was a stickler for cost and safety.

When Marshall threatened to fire him if he didn't 'shape up' he hadn't taken him seriously since no one else in the office did. Everyone knew it was Karen who ran the show. Joshua thought that as long as he pleased her, his job was safe.

But she hadn't read his report.

She hadn't even reviewed or known about it. He'd sent it in two months ago.

He had started to grow dissatisfied with the direction of the company. Writing the report had been his last ditch effort to become engaged with the vision the company said it upheld. When he hadn't heard a word from her, he'd started thinking about what options he had for the new year. He'd promised to give himself one more year before looking elsewhere.

Instead of leaving, they'd wanted to cut him loose.

He regretted believing every word she'd told him at the conference in New York. He'd had other companies, which offered larger salaries, interested in him and he'd turned them down for the chance of paving a way for the future.

Instead, after two years, she'd hidden behind a tablet telling him vague reasons for his dismissal. But then the look of surprise on her face when she heard about his report changed him. She hadn't seen his report? She hadn't been putting him off the way he thought? How could someone feel angry and relieved at the same time?

She still believed in him just as much as when she approached him at the conference years ago. He hadn't realized how much he'd depended on that faith. And now she was giving him a second chance, but only because he had a baby!

He looked at the baby again who was happily chewing on her fist. After looking through her diaper bag he'd been able to come up with one simple conclusion: She'd been abandoned on purpose. If the sight of the mother driving away, lifting up her scarf to hide her face more, hadn't been enough of a clue, inside the large diaper bag had been a birth certificate and a note saying "She's all yours."

Not "Please look after her" or "Give me to a good home" or even "Save Me" but a careless note as if the baby were stolen goods handed to someone else.

He couldn't dump her. He'd go to the police then he'd find a way to save his job on his own.

Joshua lifted his head when he heard a knock on the door. He picked up the baby and scrambled to his feet. "Come in."

Roger Sanjit, a bulky guy of thirty with a bushy beard as dark and thick as a black bear, entered. Roger was his direct supervisor and liked to keep his distance but today he had a grin on his face as he looked at the baby. "Should I even ask?"

"No."

He took seat. "You've got us all wondering."

"It's a long story."

"How did your meeting with Karen go?"

"Fine."

"Should any of us be concerned? Guys like Marshall tend to cut jobs around this time of year to make their profits look good."

"Does anyone else have a meeting scheduled?"

Roger stroked his beard. "No, just you."

Lucky him. "Then I don't think you have anything to worry about. I found out that she hadn't seen my report."

Roger paused, surprised. "Marshall assured me he'd send it along and discuss it with her."

Joshua sighed. That explained a lot.

"Nothing else then?"

"No."

Roger jumped to his feet. "Good. Meet me in the break room. I've got something to show you." He left before Joshua could argue.

Moments later, Joshua entered the empty break room

and took a seat, bouncing the baby on his knee while dreading what other meeting awaited him. Before he could imagine the worse he heard the sound of a party favor and turned to the door and saw five other colleagues, one holding a tray of cupcakes and a balloon that said "Congratulations!"

He recognized the cupcakes. They were left over from last week's celebration of those birthdays celebrated in November and December. The balloon meant some poor person had raced to the closest convenience store.

He couldn't tell them the truth. He couldn't risk the truth getting back to Karen. Instead he stared at them stunned, feeling guilty. He didn't like them making such an effort.

"You should have told us!" Harriet said. She was a smart, kind woman with thin brows and a perm that had never been in fashion.

"We know you're a private guy, but this is extreme," Donald added in a gruff tone, his cherub cheeks and shaggy hair made him look like a 70s cartoon character although he'd been born two decades later. "No pictures on your desk, no photos on your phone—"

"Don't make him feel bad," Roger said. He patted Joshua on the shoulder. "We just wanted you to know we're a team."

Joshua nodded. "Thanks."

Donald smirked. "Be honest. A one night stand came back to haunt you, right?"

Joshua didn't move and fixed him with a look. He knew they were swirling with questions, but he put on a guarded expression to keep them from prying. He put his

Glacier nickname to good use. A tense silence fell, Roger shot Donald a look and the younger man's face turned red.

Harriet cautiously leaned towards the infant with a smile. "What's the name?"

Thank God for the birth certificate. "Olivia."

"Can I hold her?"

"Sure. You can keep her if you want." His joke made them all laugh. Unfortunately he wasn't completely joking.

Because he was used to lying he answered all their questions with ease being vague enough that if he had to change his story in the future he had enough room.

Once they'd finished eating, and he got some urgent tasks done, he knew exactly what he had to do next.

$\mathcal{H}$e left the balloon in his office tied to his chair.

The only thing he held when he walked into the noisy police station, which smelled like lemon and burnt coffee, was a baby sucking on a purple pacifier.

He took a seat in the reception area waiting for the five person line to thin out before he stood there. In the back he heard someone shouting obscenities, held his breath against the whiff of body odor and liquor as an officer took a man into the back where the jail cells were and the man could find a safe place to sober up. It was only a Thursday evening he'd never expected the place to be this busy.

Finally, when he saw his chance, he raced up to the front counter and winced when a couple shouted at each other as they left the station. He turned to the clerk who looked at him with impatience, "I'm sorry," he said knowing he had wasted her time by being distracted. "I didn't expect it to be this busy."

The clerk rolled her eyes. "There are some people who celebrate from Thanksgiving until New Year's. What do you need?"

"I found this baby."

There was a loud crash like a chair falling before another officer said a code he didn't recognize. The clerk looked at him and said, "Give me a minute," before she disappeared.

"What's going on, hon?" a woman's voice said behind him. "Why would you want to give up your baby?"

He turned to see a brown skinned woman with curly grey hair and a brown coat with large orange buttons that hadn't been done right.

"She's not my baby."

"I saw you with her on the bus this morning."

"You couldn't have."

"Yes, you nearly left without her. I got my cousin to chase after you. We've been talking about you all day." She laughed. "Of course I remember you."

Joshua took a deep breath. "But the baby isn't mine. You only saw me with her because I picked her up at the bus stop."

The woman sent him a look.

"It's true. The mother asked me to look after her and then she left."

"Look how she sleeps in your arms."

Joshua didn't look down; although he was shocked the baby could sleep surrounded by such chaos. "Babies don't care. That's not a sign that I—"

"What's her name?"

"Olivia."

The woman nodded and he realized his mistake. "And I only know that because it's on her birth certificate."

The woman nodded again. "As it should be."

He then realized his second mistake. "I found the birth certificate in the diaper bag." But as he said the words he knew they sounded improbable. Who carries a birth certificate in a diaper bag?

She lowered her voice and rested a hand on his shoulder. "I know it can be difficult. Did the mother abandon you?"

"Yes, she just left me." He briefly closed his eyes and shook his head. "No wait, that sounds wrong. She didn't leave me, she left *her* this morning and that's why—"

"And that's painful, but you'll be fine. You don't want to give her up, you'll regret it."

"There's nothing to regret because she's not—"

The clerk returned to the counter and called out to him. "Okay, what were you telling me?" But before he could answer another officer, a young man with a buzz cut and chiseled cheekbones that could cut through steel, came from the back and walked up to the woman and said, "Aunt Clara how many times have I told you not to visit me here?" as he rebuttoned the woman's coat.

"I like coming here," Aunt Clara said in a bright voice, "and you can help this young man."

The officer sent Joshua a wary look as if trying to size up whether he was a criminal or victim. "What's the problem here?" he asked.

"No, problem," Aunt Clara said before he could speak. "He's lost and—"

"I found this baby," Joshua interrupted. "No, that's wrong. I didn't find her. She was abandoned at the bus stop. I can give you the location and—"

The man, Officer Rodriguez by the name tag, ran a hand through his hair and said, "That won't be necessary."

"I can sort of describe the mother. She's about late teens early twenties. Has short black hair. I think she had an earring. She was in a black Lincoln. That's all I can remember."

"If this is a domestic dispute you can—"

"There's nothing domestic about it. I don't know who she is or where she went. All I know is that I don't want to be stuck with her kid."

"When did this happen?"

"This morning."

The officer looked at his watch. "And you're just coming in now?"

"I had to get to work, I was already running late and then I had things to do." He looked down at Olivia. "She's fine. I fed her, she's got a clean diaper. She'll probably want to eat again in another hour or two and—" He stopped when they sent him a significant look. "It's not like that. I just got her on a schedule for one day. It's luck. After nearly nine hours I'm done." He held the baby out. "Take her."

Officer Rodriguez did and the baby started to cry. Aunt Clara sent him a knowing look before she said something to the man in Spanish.

Joshua shook his head. "It doesn't prove anything."

The officer handed the baby back to him and the baby started to settle. The little traitor.

Aunt Clara nodded satisfied. "By this age babies get wary of strangers."

Joshua sighed. "I *am* a stranger. I mean I was this morning. I just have a way with babies. There's nothing special about it." He set the baby down on a chair and placed the diaper bag next to her. "She has everything she needs here. I have to go now."

"It's not that simple," the officer said. "If you want to abandon your baby—"

"She's not mine. I'm telling you. I'll take a test and prove it."

"There's no need to get excited."

Joshua took another deep breath. He had to stay calm.

"He fought with his girlfriend," Aunt Clara said in Spanish, coming up with a story on her own.

"She wasn't my girlfriend," Joshua replied in the Spanish he remembered from college. He switched to English. "I don't know who she is—"

The baby started to wave her hands in the air and cry. They looked at him.

Joshua held up his hands in surrender. "She's not mine. I swear." He noticed the pacifier on the chair beside her. "See? She spat it out. That's why she's upset." He picked it up, quickly put it in his mouth to clean it and put it back in her mouth. Or at least tried, she turned her head and continued to cry. "Why are you doing this to me?" he said in a whispered plea. The baby's cries grew louder.

He shoved the pacifier in his pocket and turned back to the pair. "She's probably fussy because she's hungry."

They continued to look at him.

He thought of running. Leaving her there. They didn't know his name. Damn he should have kept his knit cap on. The police station probably had cameras. He thought of his face spread online and posted on utility poles with the words 'Wanted' written above his photo for everyone to see.

The older woman picked up the crying infant whose cries had turned into a wail. She held the baby out to him then said a bunch of words to him in rapid Spanish that he didn't understand.

Joshua looked at the officer pleading for his understanding. "What did she say?"

The officer shrugged. "I have no idea. I don't speak Spanish. She just does it to annoy me."

He turned back to Aunt Clara who held the baby out with insistence. With a sigh he walked up to a screaming Olivia and took her. To his genuine annoyance she stopped crying. He looked at the two smug faces and shook his head. He snatched the diaper bag and slung it over his shoulder, ready to find another precinct. "I know what it looks like, but I'm really not—"

"Rodriguez!" a voice shouted from the back.

"I've got to go," the officer said.

"If you find a baby floating in the Christine River you know why," Joshua said in Spanish.

Officer Rodriguez's gaze turned cold. "And if I do I'll know who to look for."

Joshua grinned he'd said the other statement in Spanish and Rodriguez had no trouble understanding him. "No, Spanish, huh?" he said in English.

It took the officer a moment to realize his mistake and swear.

"I'm used to being lied to," Joshua said.

Officer Rodriguez swore again before he said, "Listen, I want to help, but this really isn't the place for a baby. We can call Child Services, but it will take a while for them to get here." He pulled a business card out of his pocket. "But if you're really in trouble, there is someone you can reach." He handed him the card.

"What did your aunt say? The speed and accent are beyond me."

The officer shrugged. "Fair enough. She said that you're a special person. That you're a gift to this child and she's a gift to you. Don't turn away from it. Accept all the heavens have to offer."

Joshua smiled at Aunt Clara and nodded. "Thank you," he said but he didn't believe a word she'd said. He wasn't special and this baby was a gift he didn't need.

Joshua looked down at the address and the hours for the local Child Protection Services unit.

He had just enough time to get there before they closed.

But they'd already closed. Or rather moved. Joshua stared at the posted sign on the fourth floor door of the old office building. The building was in a part of town that had fallen into neglect. The cheery yellow sign with colorful flowers that said 'Sorry, we've Moved' did nothing to ease that feeling of desolation, as a fluorescent light bulb flickered and buzzed above.

Joshua stared down at the card Officer Rodriguez had given him wondering how old it was. Not that it mattered. He shoved the card in his pocket and turned to head down the stairs (the ride up on the elevator had been less than assuring).

His hopes lifted when he heard a door open and saw a tired looking woman, in a worn maroon pleather jacket, leave the office. He raced up to her. "Are you with Child Services?"

"Yes, but—"

He held out the baby. "Please take her. She's not mine. I found her this morning and—"

The woman held up her hand as if it had taken all the effort in the world to do so. "I can't take her right now." She motioned to the door. "As you can see this division is closed, I'm only here to clear up a few things. We've moved so—"

"But isn't this your job? To help a baby in need?"

The woman's eyes flashed. "My job? Do you want me to tell you about my caseload? I have two kids who have been living on dog food for the past three months while in their grandparents care, a ten year old so malnourished he looks like a four year old and a toddler found searching for food in a dumpster and you have the audacity to tell me what my job is? You really think my job is to make life easier for a man in a thousand dollar coat holding a baby who is not only well-fed but looks happy?"

"But I—"

"Right now I don't care. Is she in immediate danger?"

"No, but—"

"Then do me a favor. Do us all a favor and tell me your sob story *after* New Year's Day." She dug into her large handbag and pulled out a card. "January 5th you can call me directly and I will help you. Deal?"

Joshua sighed. "Deal."

"But if you realize by that time that she's not as much trouble as you think, don't be afraid to lose my number. I won't be offended." She made a brief wave of her hand. "Happy Holidays," she said before she headed to the stairs.

Three weeks. He could handle three weeks. In three

weeks' time he'd go to Child Services' new office, show that he hadn't changed his mind and prove that he wasn't the father. Then everything would get back to normal.

Joshua walked into his apartment and set the baby down on the couch.

The tears she'd shed at the police station had long dried up and she was looking around in wonder.

He folded his arms and looked her over. The woman at Child Services had been right. She did look well-fed. At least her mother had done that much. However, her nails were too long. She had already scratched her face, leaving a tiny mark, and on his face as well. Her chubby little hands liked to grab at everything.

Moment later, he placed her on his lap and she watched in fascination as he clipped her fingernails. At first she'd begun to cry but he'd made her giggle by kissing her on the cheek before doing the first cut. Once he was through, he sat her back down on the couch and stared at her again.

This wasn't good. But it wasn't exactly bad either. She had helped him keep his job. That was a plus. He'd take good care of her in the meantime and then she'd start a new life. They had a few things in common.

He hadn't been abandoned by his mother but he might as well have been. She chose to love something else instead of him—misery.

Every day was a misery to her. She hated her life and the son she had. She always wished for something different. The life her sister had created owning a boutique her husband had bought for her, instead of running a daycare.

When they'd briefly lived with her mother's younger brother, after his father had gone, Joshua had learned to get used to ducking blows. His mother never saw how her brother really was or didn't care (she had an elder brother who was a successful surgeon in New York who kept a great distance from both his younger siblings. Joshua remembered him best by the big smile he had in photographs and the holiday and birthday cards he'd send to him, stuffed with cash that his mother would take for safekeeping and never return). His Uncle had two girlfriends and three kids. Joshua had once seen him pour a little rum in one of his daughter's baby bottles to help her sleep. At least that's what he told him. Joshua didn't believe him. He rarely believed anyone. He'd learned early not to. His father was too clever. That's what his paternal grandmother told him. He later learned that meant his father had an aversion to staying on the right side of the law. His father was presently serving a second stint in prison for fraud.

"A no good Nigerian" That's what his mother liked to call her ex-husband and remind Joshua every month. She'd married "A no good Nigerian" and gotten nothing out of it. Joshua was the 'nothing'. She failed to consider the fact that she was the daughter of successful Nigerian immigrants, a first generation American who'd spent her formative years in England. That her parents were respected.

No, instead she liked to remember the Afro-

Caribbean man she didn't marry or the beautiful black Brazilian she'd met on holiday in Bermuda. The Afro-Cuban man who thought her eyes were beautiful.

Her life was ruined not only because she'd abandoned her university studies to marry a smooth-talking crook, but because, unlike her sister or older brother, she didn't have a glamorous life. She would have respected her ex-husband if she'd at least gotten financial compensation for her heartache. Others in her situation had done better, but instead of a palatial house, like one cousin whose name was only said in whispers, as well as the crooked spouse who'd managed to leave her with a tidy sum of money she wasn't too ashamed to spend, she lived in a two bedroom apartment. When there were events like weddings and naming ceremonies, she railed at the unfairness that she couldn't buy her cloth from Dubai or Switzerland, and could only manage a holiday once a year instead of three.

Joshua had once hoped he could defeat her misery. He told her that he loved her. In fourth grade, he'd hand-made a Valentine's Day card for her with lots of red and silver and gold glitter, hoping that would make the misery go away. But instead she'd looked at the card and then him and said 'So what?' before she grabbed his arm in a firm grip and told him love was for fools. That he should never fall in love with anybody or he'd end up as miserable as her.

She shattered his heart that day.

Part of him had wanted to defeat her misery and another part of him had wanted to hear her say that she loved him too. That she didn't mean that she regretted marrying his father and having him. That he was special to her.

But that day he learned he wasn't.

He took her words to heart. Love had no place in his life and he didn't miss it.

He guarded his heart at nine and let only one person breakthrough.

His mother learned early not to keep her misery to herself. She had a series of friends who would come over with their kids and sit and drink in the kitchen while the kids ran around unsupervised in the living room. Joshua took it upon himself to create some order in the apartment. He needed order when there was so much chaos elsewhere. He took charge of the kids and discovered he had a knack. He didn't know where it had come from but the kids gravitated to him and he was organized. He knew when to have meals ready, homework done, insert playtime or rest. Once, he'd been left to look after an eighteen month old, nine month old and four month old all at the same time. It had been hectic but he'd managed.

He didn't know the exact moment when his mother saw dollar signs. Before he knew it he was helping her run a daycare. He was too young to protest, only twelve, but he'd come home from school or sometimes be forced to miss days, and look after kids (help look after kids he was told, but he did most of the work when his mother wasn't around) he didn't want to complain because he didn't want her to be unhappy.

But she'd been angry and shocked when he told her he was going to university. The daycare was flourishing.

"Why would you need a degree when you have a

business like this?" she shouted at him in their newly redesigned kitchen as he washed up the dinner dishes. All summer he hadn't told her. He hadn't told her what school he'd be attending, what he planned to study. He knew she wouldn't care.

He set a plate aside on the dryer rack. "It's not my business, it's yours."

"No, it's *ours*." She rested a gentle hand on his arm. The only time she touched him was when she wanted something, so he wasn't fooled by her touch as much as he still craved it. "Something I can hand over to you and—"

He turned off the faucet and dried his hands. "I don't want it. I want something more."

Her tender tone turned bitter. "What am I supposed to do without you? Do you want to see me fail?"

"You shouldn't fail. You've got enough staff."

"So selfish, like your father," she said before she stormed away.

The day he left for university she didn't wish him well and as she'd feared, the daycare didn't survive without him.

She blamed him. She didn't speak to him for nearly five years. He still sent her cards for her birthday and holidays and sent her texts although he mostly stayed away. She always managed to be busy the few times he came around to check on her.

When he got his first professional job he sent her a cheque. Just enough to help her get by.

She started to speak to him again after that. That's when he knew the price he had to pay to keep her in his life and he was willing to pay it. With her in his life he wouldn't be alone. No one else mattered.

At times she lied and said she missed him. Especially during the winter holidays. He hated the season for that. He'd always repeat the same lie back to her and say he missed her too and then he'd send her a present—expensive and showy—so that he wouldn't have to see her. But he knew no one would truly miss him if he were to disappear. He had no friends anymore; two cousins were the only family willing to have anything to do with him. The others, and there were many others, stayed away because of his mother's moods and his father's reputation. His grandparents had passed. He was on his own.

He knelt in front of Olivia and held out his forefinger. She pulled her hand out of her mouth and he let her grab his finger in her chubby, wet grip. He wiggled his finger in a way that made her smile. When she pulled his finger to put it in her mouth, he picked her up instead and looked around his apartment. He'd have to figure out where to put her, get baby food, more diapers and she only had one change of clothing. He felt the soft touch of her cheek against his neck then felt a light stream of drool before he heard her sneeze. "You're not allowed to get a cold," he told her, wiping away the drool with his hand before cleaning his hand on his jeans.

It surprised him how much he didn't mind holding her. He usually didn't like people touching him. He'd felt the same way with Karen.

If there is anything you need let me know. More than Karen's smile or words, he remembered her touch. She'd lightly touched his hand and the sensation had surprised him.

He wasn't used to being touched without feeling tense. His mother's touch usually came with an agenda; his cousins' could be grabby. But Karen's touch had been light and surprising. The only other person whose touch had felt that natural had happened years ago one spring day on the playground.

He'd been playing alone, watched over by some aunt who was one of the many nameless adults who came and left his life, kicking a stick, wanting to stay out of the house while his parents argued, when someone said, "Wanna play?"

He turned around and saw a smiley faced black boy with large brown eyes and glasses to match. He'd never seen someone look so happy in his life that he just stared. "My name's Randall, what's yours?"

He blinked.

Randall laughed then said again, "What's your name?"

"J-Joshua."

"I like you Joshua, wanna play?"

"Sure."

Randall's smile widened, which Joshua found amazing, and Randall grabbed his hand and took him to the slides.

He loved the feel of Randall's hand. Firm and soft and kind. So very kind. He liked holding his hand and Randall felt the same. They ended up in the same kindergarten so they held hands crossing the street and while out on field trips. It was the most natural thing in the world to be so connected to his best friend. The one person he loved most in the world. He wanted to hold his hand forever until he was told he was too old to do that.

He didn't understand why.

He soon found out when he heard the ugly name for boys who didn't act right.

He hugged Randall instead. Quick, bear hugs he never got from anyone else. And it was through those hugs that he knew something was wrong when they were in college. Randall didn't smell the same. His scent, like his personality, always reminded Joshua of apricots and honey, but now there was an off odor like sawdust and he'd lost weight. When he asked him if he was okay, Randall smiled and said that sometimes he was a little tired but he was fine.

He wasn't fine.

Months later, Joshua got to hold his best friend's hand again. His hands were not as Joshua had remembered; they were now cold, long and thin. But Joshua didn't let go. He still held on as if he could transfer his warmth to Randall—restore his health to him, the health cancer was stealing away.

They laughed and talked about music, technology, girls, and the future. Randall wanted a wife and two kids (while Joshua said he'd never marry). He planned to be an elementary school teacher, even though it didn't pay well and his younger sister warned him that the profession wouldn't attract girls. Randall didn't care and Joshua didn't either. He knew his friend would make a wonderful teacher and inspire young people.

Joshua wanted to tell Randall he loved him, but he

knew it wouldn't make a difference. He could hear his mother say 'So what?' Love wasn't a magic word, it wouldn't heal him. It wouldn't make everything better and he didn't want to embarrass him. He might not feel the same.

So he held his best friend's hand until Randall finally let go.

Twenty-one was the last time he tried to hold on to anything. After Randall's death, Joshua designed his life so that he didn't really care about anyone and no one cared about him. He didn't want to be needed by anyone and a baby was the most helpless thing created. He didn't need the responsibility.

He felt Olivia sigh and he did the same. He was stuck with her for at least three weeks.

She'd helped him keep his job.

He'd keep her safe until the new year.

CHAPTER 8

A favor or an apology.

Karen looked at the plastic bag from Wing's China Palace that Marshall held in his hand and silently groaned wishing he'd used the eco-bag she'd bought him for such purchases. In spite of that small gaffe she hid a smile. She didn't believe in shaming anyone for trying their best. She was far from perfect.

They were the only two left in the office. It was her watch that told her that the day was over since her windowless office could give her no hint of the brightness of day or the darkness of night, but she was aware of the sudden stillness outside her door. There were no longer the bustling of footsteps, the sound of voices and the tapping of fingers against keyboards. When there was only the two of them it reminded her of when they'd first started 3R on his living room table discussing a grand idea. She closed her laptop and waited. "What's all this?"

Marshall took a seat and set the bag on the table. "I thought I should offer you an apology for today."

She took the carton he'd handed her. "What do you mean?"

"I put you on the spot about Akibu and I didn't mean to. I don't want to buy you out and I don't want you working with him."

"But I want to."

He sighed, annoyed. "Karen, it's time to stop this."

She opened up the carton, grabbed the reusable chopsticks she kept in her top draw and began to eat the vegetable stir fry. "I'm excited. I want a challenge like this. Remember when you first told me about your idea and—?"

Marshall dove his chopsticks into his fried rice with a frown. "Why do you have to be stuck in the past?"

His words hurt. She wasn't stuck. She always liked thinking about the moment that changed both their lives. It was also something that only they shared. It made her feel close to him. She didn't know why he always seemed irritated when she mentioned it.

She took another bite, pushing down her pain. He didn't understand her. That wasn't his fault. She had to prove to him how useful she was then he'd care and realize how special that day, all those years ago, had truly been. "I'm not changing my mind."

"Why not? You have nothing to prove."

I have everything to prove. "I'm not only doing this for you. I want to see what I can do with some of his ideas."

"You shouldn't make this business your life."

"It isn't."

He sat back in his chair looking doubtful. "When's the last time you took a vacation?"

"I don't need one."

"Or gone out on a date?"

She shifted awkwardly in her seat and mumbled. "I've been out on dates."

He shook his head. "I didn't say *if* I said *when*. Admit it. You're married to this job."

"I don't see it as a job, but as a mission. I told you that." He didn't realize how much he was hurting her. Didn't he know that being by his side was all she needed? She didn't need a vacation or another man. She wanted to help make all their dreams for the business come true. She didn't have a greater ambition than that.

But as much as his words, carelessly said but not cruel, hurt she knew he wasn't trying to cause her pain. He truly wanted to help her. That was the kind of man he was. He might not see her as a woman, but he did worry about her. Worry was something right? She could work with worry.

Worry could turn into care and then care into love. That wasn't so far a stretch.

She'd accept his apology, but she wouldn't back down.

He didn't want to remember that night when their lives had changed, but she would and she'd remember this one as a new night. A night where she was reborn as a woman who didn't want to be overlooked by him anymore.

She wanted to rise to a challenge, to take an idea and see where it led her.

CHAPTER 9

They still hadn't said anything.

Joshua sat in front of his cousins as they sat around his kitchen table and waited for their response to the baby on his lap and the explanation he'd given them, but Tilly and Frank stared at him dumbfounded.

He'd called in sick on Friday since he was not going to take Olivia with him to work again and didn't have someone to look after her. He'd spent the morning shopping for diapers, formula and bedding, he spent the afternoon trying to calm Olivia down when she got her little hand caught in a toy that he'd bought for her. He made a note to return the toy and file a complaint. After getting her to calm down, she went on, with childish, adventurous glee, to show him how much his apartment was not childproof by nearly toppling a plant, pulling down a lamp when she grabbed hold of its cord and bumping her head on his coffee table. He'd been so busy chasing after her that he forgot to pick up his car.

So he invited his cousins over for dinner hoping to get some help with the situation. He'd ordered a pizza that was getting cold. They were his only tie to his father's side of the family and unaffected by his mother's constant misery. They'd both inherited the family's dark brows, but Frank got all the height, while Tilly barely reached five feet. She made up for it by piling her long hair in a high braided bun on her head.

He was desperate to have someone believe him. And he knew they did; however, their stunned silence was starting to get to him. Was it too much to ask them to help him find someone to look after Olivia while he was at work? He was willing to pay.

"Well?" he finally said.

Frank blinked.

Tilly shook her head. "I don't know what to say."

"A baby at a bus stop," Frank said amazed.

Olivia happily slapped her hands on the table, rattling the dishes.

"Who did your sister have looking after her kids?" Joshua asked, moving his chair back so Olivia couldn't reach the table.

"Mom did it mostly."

"Do you think you could convince her?" Joshua said hopeful, although he and his aunt weren't close. "She'll only have to look after her on the weekdays, while I'm at work. I'll pay a competitive rate and—"

"I can ask," Tilly said, "but I'm not sure."

"Or if you could do it..." He suggested knowing she worked from home as a freelance web designer.

"I'm no good with babies."

"She's not that hard."

"Couldn't you take vacation time?" Tilly said.

Joshua shook his head. "I was about to get fired, I can't take a holiday right now."

"You're really going to keep her?"

He could feel Olivia getting antsy so he grabbed her pacifier from the counter and gave it to her before he returned to the table. "I don't have a choice. It's only until the new year."

"The woman just left her?" Frank asked again.

"Yes."

"And the police don't believe she's not yours?"

Joshua nodded.

Frank frowned. "Think the mother will change her mind and come looking?"

"I doubt it. She left a note and a birth certificate. The only address on it is the California hospital where the baby was born."

"You're lucky she's black." Frank started to laugh. "Imagine you going around with a white baby."

Joshua frowned seeing no humor in the situation. "Then I wouldn't be in this mess."

"What do you mean?"

"It would have been easier for people to believe that she wasn't mine."

Frank quickly sobered. "That's true." He picked up a pizza slice.

"That's not the point. If your mother won't help, do you know of a reliable service I could call?"

"I think it's a risk," Tilly said. "What if they want more information than you can provide?"

"I can bluff my way through anything."

"What will you do at your job in the new year when you don't have her anymore?"

"I'll say my girlfriend missed her and we agreed she'd take care of her."

Tilly feigned a shiver. "You are a good liar."

He wasn't offended because it was true. He'd make his boss and the others believe what he wanted them to. "It'll work."

"Why do you care? I thought you'd started hating this job anyway."

"I never said I hated it."

"You said you were unhappy."

"I've changed." Especially now that he knew Karen hadn't seen his report. He was eager to see how she would respond to what he'd written. "I want to stay there."

"What if you grow attached to her?"

He shook his head then handed Frank a napkin when a mushroom dropped on his light blue shirt, smearing it with tomato sauce. "I won't."

"Three week's a long time."

"I won't." He frowned at Frank who was making the stain worse by rubbing it. "Dab it and—"

"You never know," Tilly said.

He shifted his attention back to her. "I won't."

Tilly looked at Olivia with new interest. "You know you could use her in another way."

Joshua held up his hand, the expression on his cousin's face made him uneasy. "I'm not interested."

"Go to the park with her. Single dads can attract a lot of attention."

"I don't care about attention. I care about keeping a roof over my head. Feeding myself, you know the basics and a job does that."

She looked around the kitchen where he'd covered all the electrical outlets, mopped the grey tiled floor and locked the wood cabinets. She opened her mouth to say something when her gaze fell on an invitation sitting on the counter. She reached out and picked it up. "You haven't even opened it."

"I know."

She turned it over. "It looks like a wedding invitation."

Joshua nodded. "Because it is."

She looked at him surprised. "And you're not opening it?"

Frank nudged her with his elbow. "Leave him alone. He's got enough on his mind."

"But isn't he even curious?"

"I'm not going so there's no need," Joshua said.

She flashed an impish grin. "Can I open it?"

Joshua shrugged. He didn't care about her curiosity. He knew who the invitation was from—Randall's sister. She was getting married next fall and wanted him to be there. He didn't know why. He didn't know why she and her family continued to keep in touch. Why they continued to invite him to dinners and barbecues. He didn't know why they felt obligated. Part of him wondered if they wanted him in their lives to remember Randall by, but he knew he was a poor substitute.

Randall was light and he darkness. He hoped by his silence they'd learn to leave him alone.

Tilly opened the envelope and whistled. "Ooo...looks expensive." She waved the invitation. "Why aren't you going to this?"

"Why would I go?" He watched Frank reach for a second slice of pizza pleased it wouldn't go to waste since he'd lost his appetite.

"Because you were invited? Isn't this Randall's sister?"

"Yes."

"Then you *have* to go."

"No, I don't. I'll hardly know anyone."

"Knowing the bride is pretty much enough and her parents. If you don't RSVP soon you'll miss your chance."

"I won't."

"You might change your mind."

"I don't know why she'd want me there." He didn't know why he'd kept the invitation instead of throwing it away.

"She likes you."

Joshua snatched the invitation from her. "Are you willing to help me or not?"

"Do you know why you were about to get fired?"

"The president hates me and there were supposedly complaints about my personality. That I'm condescending and not a team player."

He'd learned to keep to himself. It was easier, safer, less painful that way. Do your job and leave. That had been his motto. He'd learned that lesson well.

"When people don't know you, you can come off a little...standoffish."

"I don't really care. All that matters now is I have a chance to prove myself. Maybe get a pay raise or promotion, then it will be over."

Tilly thought for a moment before she said, "I'll do it if you go to the wedding."

"I'm not going," he said in a bored tone. "Try again."

"At least RSVP."

"I'm not going."

"Why do you have to be so stubborn?"

"If you won't help me, I'll just—"

"She'll do it," Frank said. He stood. "Come on, let's go."

Tilly left with her brother, annoyed. She'd been so close to getting Joshua to come out of his shell and her brother had ruined it. Somehow she felt that going to Randall's sister's wedding was important. "What's the rush?" she asked her brother as he hurried to the parking lot. She wrapped her coat tighter against a swift cold wind. The trees around the complex were dotted with white holiday lights and large red ribbons wrapped around light poles.

"This is a great opportunity. Did you hear how much he was offering?"

Tilly rolled her eyes. "Everything isn't about money."

"It is when the rent's coming due."

"This month's been paid."

"Actually it wasn't."

Tilly stopped walking and glared at him. "What do you mean?"

Frank kept walking to her blue Prius.

She ran up to him and spun him around. "What do you mean?"

He had the grace to look sheepish. It was an expression he used well. It had gotten him out of trouble numerous times. It was that expression that had gotten her to believe it would be a good idea to share an apartment with him since he was finishing his graduate degree and their father had lost patience with him staying at home and not working a full-time job. Instead, he was working as a freelance grant writer. "I had a bill I needed to pay so I borrowed the rent money hoping I'd be able to cover it later, but then I didn't get as many jobs this month as I'd hoped to and—"

Tilly held up her hand. "This is the last time I let you take care of it. From now on it's direct deposit." She sighed. "You really are a mess sometimes."

Frank didn't argue as he got inside her car. He picked up the book he'd left on his seat. It was some self-help book Tilly had been going on about called, *Being Real, Staying Real.* She was a devotee of the author's podcast too, which talked about the power of inner fortitude and changing your life through good thoughts. He tossed the book into the backseat. Who cared about things like that when your life was broken? He felt bad. He felt bad most of the times. Bad that he wasn't a better brother to Tilly, that he'd disappointed his parents, that he always seemed to be short on cash. But he was tired of feeling that way and visiting Joshua had given him an idea. An idea that could change everything.

Frank could barely contain his excitement once he closed the door to his bedroom. This was his chance to make serious money. He walked past his desk that was littered with the corpses of unopened late bill notices. He wasn't a religious man, but the opportunity Joshua had given them could make him a believer.

He looked out his tiny window at the shopping center across the street. He hadn't been able to buy his sister anything for two Christmases in a row, but this year would be different.

This was going to be the best holiday ever. He was so excited he could hardly keep himself still. He saw all their problems ending. He pulled out his cell phone and said, "Guess what? I've got a baby for you."

CHAPTER 10

Incredible.

Karen sat on her living room couch unable to believe what she'd just read. Joshua's report was better than she could have imagined. How had this missed her? Why hadn't his supervisor let her know? His ideas were incredible! To think that she'd almost lost a goldmine like this? From now on she'd let everyone know they had a direct line to her; she couldn't let an oversight like this happen again.

She set his report aside and briefly looked over his performance review again. Something had to be fixed. None of the numbers could accurately depict what he brought to the company. She'd deal with that later, first she had to choose one of these projects and see how she could implement it. Some were too outlandish, others outrageously expensive, but she felt that with an adjustment they could move forward on a smaller task.

She hoped that he would be amenable. These next

three weeks would be crucial.

That Monday she met with Joshua in her office instead of the conference room. She felt a change of scene would make him less...on edge. She was wrong. He still entered the room like a warrior ready to do battle, she knew she would have to work extra hard to get him to relax and trust her.

But as she watched him take a seat, she had a sense that there were few people he trusted. He wore a crisp white shirt under a green sweater and dark blue jean and looked about as domesticated as a crocodile. She wondered who had managed to get past the wall she sensed surrounded him. She swallowed hard and rubbed her hands together. She'd once been bold enough to convince him to leave a larger company that turned plastic bottles into luxury bags and accessories, and join her much smaller company that created their own materials; she would become that ambitious woman once again.

There was too much on the line for them to be at odds with each other. They needed to work as a unit as soon as possible.

"I see you were able to get a sitter today," she said hoping to break the ice.

"Hmm."

"I heard your team gave you a little party." She set a small, fuzzy brown teddy bear on the desk. It wore a red shirt and had the name 'Olivia' stitched on its stomach with green thread. "Here's my contribution."

"You didn't have to."

"I know."

He nodded but didn't touch the toy. "Thanks."

She inwardly sighed. He was still as distant as ever. "I've spoken with your supervisor and told him that you'll be working with me for the next several weeks on a special project. You'll report directly to me with any questions or concerns. No one else must know what we're doing."

"Okay."

She'd expected him to protest about the secrecy or ask questions about the project so his ready agreement flustered her. She'd prepared for a fight that didn't come. She glanced around the room, briefly wishing she had a window from which to gaze out and collect her thoughts. But instead she was surrounded by four walls and had to face a man's dark piercing gaze. She cleared her throat. "Right...okay." She lifted her tablet and looked at some of the notes, before she had the image transferred to the blank left wall so that he could see them too. "I was looking over your report and I must say that it's impressive."

He nodded.

"However, only a few of your ideas would be feasible at this moment."

He nodded again.

Karen hesitated unsure of his impassive features. It was strange having him so amenable. "Don't you have anything to say?"

"No."

"You don't disagree?"

He kept his gaze on the image. "You haven't said anything that I disagree with yet."

"Okay." She circled two ideas in red. "I'd like to work

on one of these two. I thought it would be only fair that you choose which one you'd like to do first."

He pointed to one. It involved developing an alternative source for one of the solvents currently being used. "I don't like our dependency on this product. A main ingredient is a particular leaf and I've heard rumors of a tiny infestation that may be in the region where it is grown. If it spreads and wipes out this particular leaf we will have no alternatives to turn to. However, there is another leaf that has similar properties that we should explore."

Her heart leaped with joy. She'd wanted to work on that one too. She liked the idea of a preventative measure instead of waiting for the worse to happen which seemed to be the way Marshall liked to handle things. "Great. We'll get started on this right away."

"But I also think there's something else to consider."

"What?"

"Rapid growth."

She leaned forward not sure she'd heard him. "I'm sorry?"

"Last year during the holidays we almost didn't make our production quota because we had more orders than expected late September into the holiday season. I fear we'll be making the same mistake this year. I've spoken to the marketing division and they are doing a major push this year, however I think we're reaching beyond our capacity instead of fulfilling the orders for our main clients first. I don't think we should be focusing on gaining more for the following year."

He had surprised her again. She'd known Marshall had wanted to expand marketing, but she hadn't been aware of any particular plans that had already been put into place. She felt ashamed that she hadn't had a handle on all that was going on in the company. She'd been so busy focusing on managerial issues and putting out little fires that she hadn't paid attention to the health of the business as a cohesive unit. As long as they were making a profit, keeping to their mission and hitting their targets, she let Marshall take the lead without question.

She bit her lip and stared at the tablet half wanting to pretend that she knew and defend whatever idea Marshall had, and half wanting Joshua to tell her even more of what she'd missed. She turned to Joshua and saw him watching her in an intense way that made her blush. He was waiting for her response. She decided to push her embarrassment aside. "Do you have the marketing campaign?"

He gave her a curt nod, but she could tell that he was pleased. What he showed her made her stomach drop. It was an extensive national campaign.

She stared at it horrified. She and Marshall had agreed to keep their reach within the closest five states in order to keep track of distribution and travel. If they had clients on the west coast their costs would soar, also they didn't have enough resources on hand to double their efforts if, during the holidays, there was a rush of orders into the new year. Such an over demand could put them in the red for months. Not to mention the harm it would do to their reputation if they upset clients.

Because 3R also provided material to designers whose schedules were set, accommodating them was their utmost priority. This new push could possibly not only overextend them, but alienate the clients they already had, use up the resources they had, put too much inventory in the warehouse with rush orders, change the shipping schedule and lead to a host of other ills.

"Fortunately, the launch has been delayed," she heard Joshua say between the ringing in her ears.

She felt the knot in her chest ease. "It has?"

He nodded. "By two months. However, it's scheduled to go live the first week in January. A New Year's extravaganza."

The knot in her chest returned. "Why was it delayed before?"

"There was a concern that there wouldn't be enough products. I was already concerned about the infestation and let them know that until that was addressed we would only have enough products for our present clients."

"Really? Then things are worse that I thought. We need to find a new solvent and—" She stopped when Joshua bit his lip then shook his head. "What is it?"

"I lied."

"You lied?"

"About the infestation. I exaggerated its reach. It's something to consider for the future, but it's not a reality yet." He sighed. "If you want to fire me this is probably a good reason."

"I'm not going to fire you. What did you do?"

"I knew that we needed time. Roger felt the same but after a meeting with Marshall we couldn't get him to understand the importance of taking a step back so I talked to the head of development and marketing and we agreed that a delay would be in everyone's best interest. So I came up with a reason for it. However, if this campaign goes live next month we'll still be in trouble. I'm not saying that the campaign is wrong—"

"It's just wrong for right now."

He nodded.

She pounded the desk annoyed. "I don't understand why Marshall thinks more about making money than making a difference." She caught herself and sent Joshua a look. She had to make sure she and Marshall appeared as a solid partnership. "Not that he always thinks that way. He knows how important our mission is."

Joshua nodded again but didn't reply.

Karen wracked her brain. She would have to take the lead and stop the campaign. She knew that money had already been spent and Marshall would hate to see it wasted, but it would save them in the long run. "I will take care of this. You can rest assured. In the interim we'll look at the possible alternative solvent base, which could lead to much more. Of course we don't have to have everything in place, just a presentation to show to Marshall."

Joshua shook his head.

"What?"

"Why would we present it to him?"

Karen stammered through her words shocked by the question. "B-because he's the president."

"But you're the brains."

She smiled. "You don't need to flatter me."

He frowned. "I'm not. Everyone knows you're the reason this business is a success."

"You're new here."

He lifted his brows amused. "I've been here two years."

"I know, but that hasn't given you time to see the full role that Marshall plays. He has a sharp mind for business."

"But not development, research, production, changing market trends, customer retention—"

"Of course you have a right to your opinion, but I disagree," Karen cut in, feeling irritated. Marshall may not be as sharp as Joshua, but he was not the incompetent man he was trying to paint him to be. "I wouldn't be here without Marshall's sharp insight, compassion and intellect."

Joshua nodded but this time she knew he did the motion to appease her rather than to show her that he agreed. She didn't care. He was just an engineer. He didn't know how to read people the way she did. Perhaps he was worried that all his hard work would fail. Perhaps he was still concerned about his job. Yes, that had to be it. She felt some of her annoyance fade. He was on edge because of that. How could she have been so unsympathetic? He was worried about his job and his daughter. She'd be just as defensive in his position.

"My job is also on the line," she said.

"What?"

She laughed at his stunned expression. "I won't go into the gory details but if this project doesn't work I'll have to accept giving up some stake of the business." Not everything at least. She and Marshall had renegotiated the agreement instead of a buyout.

"But you're partners."

"Partners split. I only told you so that you can be assured that I don't plan to lose anything. Together we're going to take 3R in another exciting direction."

"I'm sorry, but you misunderstood me."

"What?"

"I'm not saying that we don't present our ideas to Marshall, but you need to do it in a way to let him think it was his idea and that it will make money. You don't need to ask for permission on this. That's what I meant by you being the brains."

He made sense but he also made her nervous. Persuade Marshall by using his ego against him? Was that right?

"He does it to you," Joshua said as though reading her mind.

"I'm sorry?"

Joshua sat back and stroked his goatee, the sheen in his gaze seeming to change to a charmingly seductive leer. "Karen, you really are too sentimental," Joshua said imitating Marshall's manner and tone. He straightened and returned his voice to normal. "You shouldn't let him talk to you like that."

Karen blinked trying to adjust to the abrupt change in Joshua's appearance. When he'd imitated Marshall she saw a sexy side she hadn't noticed before. While he didn't have Marshall's finesse, he was a good looking guy.

But his looks weren't important. She mentally shook her head, trying to clear her thoughts before she said, "That's just his way."

"He shouldn't personally attack you."

"He doesn't."

"Every time you disagree with him he makes it personal. If you don't believe me listen to what he says the next time you say something he doesn't like. He's a little afraid of you." A sly grin touched the corner of his mouth. "You're a lot stronger than you think."

The way he looked at her made her cheeks burn. He made her feel powerful, as if she could conquer anything. His grin also made her feel a little bit naughty as if they were two children up to no good.

She quickly glanced away, no longer feeling as if the windowless room was confining. It felt bigger somehow. A strange, giddy feeling of anticipation enveloped her.

Usually she dreaded making Marshall upset but this time she felt inspired. Challenged. She liked the idea of a challenge. She felt as if Joshua had lit a fire within her that had been snuffed out.

She met his gaze again. "We'll see."

His grin widened, but he didn't reply.

He didn't need to. That grin said it all. It said they were finally a team. He had confided in her about his lie and she'd forgiven him. They could trust each other.

She had too much to think about to even get started on their new project yet. "Um..."

Joshua stood. "I'll wait for you to get back to me after you talk to marketing and Marshall." He walked to the door.

"Thanks," she said glad that he understood but a little hurt that he was leaving her gift behind. But she didn't want to pressure him to take it if it made him feel uncomfortable.

The moment the door closed, she tucked it in her desk drawer and was about to close it shut when she heard a soft knock on the door. "Come in."

Joshua walked in and said, "Sorry I forgot—" He stopped and stared at her desk. It took a second to realize that he'd returned for the bear.

"Oh, of course," Karen said quickly taking the bear out and handing it to him.

He took it and their fingers touched.

Just the tips.

It shouldn't have felt like lighting.

And she suddenly heard bells ringing.

Bells that made her think of sleigh rides and cuddling up next to somebody warm on a winter day.

"Is that your favorite song?" he asked.

Karen frowned confused by the question. "What?"

"Jiggle bells."

Karen blinked before she realized why she'd heard bells. The sound of bells weren't in her head. They were real! The festive song *Jingle Bells* played from her cell phone happily filling the room. She'd set the song to play as an alarm to make sure their meeting didn't last too long. She turned it off embarrassed. "Only one of them."

Joshua nodded then waved the stuffed bear in his hand. "Thanks again for this."

"No problem," she said and meant it. Buying a gift for a baby had been easy. She knew talking to marketing would be more of a challenge. But her biggest obstacle was facing Marshall and telling him that his idea wasn't going to happen.

CHAPTER 11

"Y ou did what?!"

Karen had never seen Marshall cry before, but the moment she told him what she'd done he looked at her near tears. She'd met with him in his office with his favorite iced coffee and a muffin. Neither of which he'd touched as he stared at her. But she knew she couldn't back down. "Listen to why—"

"You did what?!"

He was out of his chair now glaring down at her. She crossed her legs and calmly said, "I canceled the marketing campaign indefinitely."

"Why?"

"We had to," she said in a soft voice.

In response his voice grew louder. "No, we didn't. Do you know how much money's already been spent?"

Karen sent him a cutting look. "Yes, and there are more bills to pay since you signed a number of contracts without letting me know."

For a moment he looked chagrined but the expression quickly disappeared. "Why did you do it?"

"Sit down and I'll tell you."

He folded his arms.

She waited.

He softly swore then sat and took a large swallow of his coffee.

"We're not ready yet," Karen said. "We're too small."

He set the cup down. "Exactly and we need to grow."

"In the future but not now. Bigger isn't always better."

"What we're doing is hot right now and—"

"I don't care whether we're hot or not. I'm in this for the long haul. Not to be some buzzy trend on social media or elsewhere."

"But timing is everything." He leaned forward, his beautiful eyes pleading with her to understand. "This could be a perfect opportunity to let more people know what we're capable of."

"The right people already know that. We have a solid client base willing to work with us. I believe that with patience we will see a steady growth we can support instead of something that could get out of hand and sink us."

Marshall sat back and sniffed in derision. "We? Is that the royal 'we'? Are you the queen now, huh? I listened to you when you didn't want investors."

"Because then we'd be beholden to them."

"Beholden? Don't be so dramatic. With more cash we could have been further along."

"With someone else running the show."

He tapped the desk with his forefinger. "You also made sure marketing is barely half the size of R&D."

"Because research and development is our foundation."

"Fine." He shrugged, lowered his gaze and poked the muffin with his finger. "I guess my opinion doesn't matter. You're running a one woman show."

That was unfair. For the first time he sounded and looked like a petulant child. How come she'd never noticed that before? And how dare he suggest she was acting like royalty. That was a cruel slight. He was putting her down. He never spoke to the other guys like that. He'd argue facts and figures. They were never emotional, dramatic, reckless, hysterical. Things he sometimes called her. But she didn't care what he said since she'd stopped an impending disaster.

"When I saw the report Joshua showed me and the possible cost that an unexpected rush could cause I knew I had to do something."

"Akibu?" Marshall's voice cracked. He picked up the muffin and she saw his grip tighten enough around it that she half expected he'd squeeze the muffin's top off. "You spoke to Akibu about this?"

"And marketing of course."

He carefully set the muffin down and wiped his hands on a napkin. He kept his voice and gaze low. "I thought you were only supposed to be working on a project."

"We thought that we would focus on this first."

He met her eyes. "Are you his partner or mine?"

"Marshall."

"I can't believe you sided with him like that."

He looked really distressed. Did he think she was trying to undermine him? Didn't he see how valuable the kind of insight Joshua had given them would be to them both?

"If you'd listened to what he'd had to say you would have come around too. I have just as every right to be upset as you. Why didn't you tell me about this campaign?"

"You were busy."

"I wasn't that busy. And why didn't I ever get Joshua's report?"

"I told you, I didn't want to waste your time. It's a bunch of crazy ideas."

"Not all of them. And did you ever tell him you were going to get rid of him?"

Marshall paused. "No, of course not. W-why would you say that?"

"He thought he overheard it but I told him it was likely a misunderstanding."

Marshall leaned forward and pointed at her. "This is what I've been afraid of."

"Afraid?"

"He's planting lies to divide us."

"He wouldn't do that," she said then hesitated when she remembered he'd lied before to delay the marketing campaign. Something in her expression, put Marshall at ease and he began to smile. "You sense it to, don't you? He's an ambitious man. You don't know what he's capable of."

❄

That's what made him interesting, Karen thought as she left Marshall's office.

She felt good sending Joshua a text with a smile to let him know that everything was fine. He didn't return the smile, but by his simple 'good' reply she could tell that he was pleased.

That gave her courage to approach Marshall again two days later to address another of her concerns. However, this time she entered his office with something that surprised him.

He stared at the object she'd placed on his desk. "What's that?"

"A piggybank." It wasn't exactly a piggybank it was in the shape of a pink high heel shoe but was designed with the same intention.

Marshall looked at her with impatience. "I know what it *is*. I want to know what's it for?"

"I want to see if we can have a fifteen minute discussion without you putting me down."

"I never do that."

"Anytime you say things such as 'you are...' 'childish' or 'silly' you have to put in a quarter."

He sniffed. "Who carries around change anymore?"

"I know you do. Especially for the vending machine." He had a weakness for chocolate bars and caramel bites.

"You're being ridiculous."

She pointed to the bank.

"I'm not going to play your childish game."

She pointed again.

He reached into his pocket, then dropped two quarters in and swore. "What's gotten into you?"

"I just noticed a bad habit of yours and I want to help correct it. Can we have a discussion without it being personal? You can disagree with my ideas, my logic, but not me."

"You're not acting like yourself."

"Do you want to have this meeting or not?"

He sighed. "You're wearing my patience thin this week. I think you're pushing it."

She took a seat. "I think I'm on a roll actually."

"Are you here to tell me another way you're going to cost me money?"

She lifted a brow. "You? I didn't realize that the marketing campaign came out of your personal funds."

"Never mind. What do you want?"

"I'm redesigning the performance review tool."

He sent her a look. "Because of *him*, right?"

"No. Because it's the right thing to do."

Marshall flashed a sour grin. "Then who am I to stop you?"

CHAPTER 12

She looked like sunshine.

When Joshua entered Karen's office after receiving a text that she wanted to speak to him, at first he stopped in the doorway and stared. She sat behind her desk holding up a bright pink high heeled shoe with a big smile on her face. He felt the true warmth of that smile; it was like the soft beating rays of a spring sun over a valley. Open, wide, welcoming. Her smile reminded him so much of Randall that he almost smiled back.

"It worked," she said.

He closed the door behind him and took a seat, confused. She'd already let him know that the campaign had been stopped, the past two days had been about budget cuts to weather the financial loss to come. "What worked?"

"I did what you said and it worked."

"I forgot what I said."

"I had a meeting with Marshall and first he didn't

listen, but then when he found out how serious I was he did." She sighed pleased. "I feel so refreshed."

"I'm happy for you."

She shook the shoe and he heard coins clink together. "I even made some money."

"Money?"

"Every time Marshall made an unflattering personal comment he had to put in a quarter."

"Bet he ran out of them."

Karen looked at him surprised. "How did you know?"

"Just a guess."

She set the bank on the table with a flourish. "It's yours."

"Why? Treat yourself. You deserve it."

"I think you deserve it. I wouldn't have done this without you."

He shook his head. "I only made a suggestion."

"Use it to buy Olivia something. Please." She pushed it towards him. "I won't take no."

He felt guilty taking it. "I'd feel silly going around with a shoe like that."

"Oh, right. Fine. I'll give you the money later."

He nodded hoping she'd forget. "Thanks."

"He's seeing me in an entirely different way."

"When are you going to tell him you love him?"

She stared at him stunned. "How did you know?"

Joshua softly swore. What had made him ask her that? It was a question he'd sometimes wondered about but had the good sense to keep to himself. What had made him blurt it out like that? Usually it didn't bother him how her gaze grew hazy and soft when she spoke about Marshall but today something about the tone in her voice irked him.

And what did she mean 'How did you know?'At times her naiveté stunned him. How could a woman so smart, be so daft sometimes? He was embarrassed that she thought her feelings were a secret. It wasn't like him to be so reckless. He should have kept his mouth shut. "Sorry. Not my place."

"You probably think I'm a coward."

"I don't think anything."

"I seriously doubt that," Karen said with a laugh.

"I'll rephrase that. I don't think I have anything to say that I want to share with you."

"Fair enough. But if we were friends."

"We're not."

"If we were—"

"And you weren't my boss and you didn't have the power to retaliate with—"

She lowered her head and held up her hand. "I would never retaliate because of an honest opinion."

"Let's change the subject."

She lifted her head, eager to share. "There's so much at stake you see. I don't want to ruin what we have."

Joshua shook his head, resisting the urge to plug his ears. "I'm not listening."

"But I know I can't live like this forever. I have to face my fears."

"Still not listening."

"I'd always wanted to walk into Marshall's office one day and surprise him by—"

Joshua jumped to his feet. "I'm definitely not listening to that."

Karen laughed. "I'm kidding. Sit down." After he cautiously did she said, "I know, I'm being unfair. But you've got me curious since you discovered my secret."

Joshua sat back and sighed. "Karen?"

"Yes."

"It's not a secret."

She blinked several times. "It's not?"

"No, everyone knows how you feel."

She widened her eyes. "Even *him*?"

Joshua hesitated. She looked so devastated he regretted his honesty. But he hated her living a delusion. "I can't speak for him, he may not see it, but I just thought you should know."

"You think I'm pathetic, don't you?" She held up her hand. "Wait, I don't think I want to know the answer."

Joshua paused and clasped his hands together, studying her. "Are you sure?"

"No." She folded her arms. "Okay, tell me the truth."

"Even if it hurts?"

She nodded.

"I think Marshall's an idiot."

She stared at him. For a moment he thought he'd gone too far. She adored Marshall. Would she shout at him for insulting her beloved? She always got defensive anytime he said anything less than complimentary about him. But she'd wanted the truth and he felt she deserved it. Before the silence became painful Karen covered her mouth and started to giggle. Joshua breathed a sigh of relief.

"That's the sweetest thing someone's ever said to me."

He didn't understand her reaction. Sweet? He wasn't trying to be sweet. "It's true."

"Yes, I guess you're right. He's an idiot for not noticing how great I am."

Joshua paused. No, he truly thought Marshall was an idiot but if she preferred to see it that way, that was fine too.

"You've really made my day. I'll pay for dinner."

"Dinner?"

"Yes, we're going to have to work overtime if we want to get this project in a suitable shape before the new year. I know you like working late hours." When she saw him hesitate she quickly said, "Oh, I'm sorry I forgot. Olivia."

"Right."

She bit her lip. "Is it really just you?"

He didn't misunderstand her. He knew she wondered if Olivia's mother was in the picture. "Yes, it's just Olivia and me." At least that wasn't a lie.

"I realize it's hard to find someone in the day let alone at night."

"I have someone who's helping me out."

"Good, but I'll try to be more considerate. Do you think we could meet tomorrow afternoon for a working lunch? Anything on your schedule?"

"No," he said annoyed with himself for how much he looked forward to it.

CHAPTER 13

"So what's on your mind?"

His father seemed to have a sixth sense when something was wrong. Marshall never regretted one of his surprise visits. They sat in a private booth at his father's favorite Indian restaurant, the fragrance of curry and masala floated through the air. He told him about Karen and the canceled marketing plan and the changes to the performance review. As much as he wanted to he didn't tell him about Akibu. That was a private matter he never wanted his father to know about.

His father sat back after Marshall had finished speaking and Marshall waited in anticipation for the advice he would give him. His father was a good listener but an even better strategist.

"Karen is a very special woman," he finally said.

Marshall frowned disappointed. That's it? That was all he had to say? He'd expected more than that. "I know."

"One who needs to be handled with care."

"I think she's being influenced."

His father shook his head. "No, I think she's telling you something."

"She's telling me she wants to take over the business."

"No. She's telling you that she's not being valued."

"I value her," he mumbled, scooping up his basmati rice.

"She wants a bigger role, to stretch her wings. It's in your best interest she doesn't stretch them too far and fly away."

His heart began to pound. That was his greatest fear. "I know that."

"What do you plan to do?"

"I'm letting her show me some new project she's working on." He didn't mention the silly challenge he'd offered her. "I think she's bored."

"I think you need to rattle her a little more than that."

"Rattle her?"

His father nodded. "It's about time you settled down, don't you think?"

Marshall shifted in his seat not understanding the new direction the conversation had taken. "I've been considering it."

"Stop considering it and make it official. She's telling you that she's starting not to trust you. You can't be the carefree bachelor all your life with a woman like that."

The fog finally cleared from his thoughts. Of course! His image. He needed to shake it up so that she could start respecting him more as she had in the past. "I see."

His father measured him with a look. "I hope you do.

You're the captain. Don't let her forget that you're the one who came up with the raw idea and backing."

"Right." His father's words gave him the courage to share more. "There's this man."

His father's voice sharpened. "Is he a threat?"

"Yes."

"How long has she been seeing him?"

Marshall laughed. He found the thought of Karen dating amusing and that his father would make such a mistake was charmingly old fashioned. A woman like Karen didn't do things like that. "She isn't seeing anyone. The man I'm talking about works for the company, but she's taken a shining to him. He's clever and persuasive."

"Then it's important that you make your move now before it's too late."

Before it's too late. His father's words echoed in his ears as he left the restaurant. He had to make his move. He had to rattle her. He had to do something now. Akibu was going to destroy his life if he didn't stop him.

Akibu could topple all he'd built. Marshall sat in his car and looked up at a holiday wreath decorating a pole. He didn't feel in the holiday spirit. He felt cold inside. Today was the third time Akibu had gotten Karen to act out of character. She would never have stopped the campaign otherwise. His hold on her was tightening. He was trying to steal her away and once he did, he'd get his hands on the business next.

Before it's too late.

What if he already was? What if he wasn't able to rattle Karen enough to change her mind about what the company needed?

Don't forget that you came up with the bulk of the idea and the backing. Marshall remembered his father's words with guilt. Because it wasn't true.

CHAPTER 14

Eighteen years ago...

He felt like he was dying. He couldn't come up with any ideas and he'd waited too late. The project was due tomorrow. He knew his father was spending money on this private school and his grades hadn't been stellar. He'd hoped things would have changed by his junior year, but he was still struggling for every grade he got. He really didn't think it was fair that he had to pick up his niece from daycare just because his sister couldn't get off work in time.

But his mother had promised him his favorite banana pancakes if he did and he wasn't above being bribed.

He'd been to the tiny daycare on the third floor of an apartment complex before so when he entered the room he wasn't surprised to see the owner's serious looking kid wiping the face of some wailing toddler and his nerdy friend sitting in a circle with five little kids who were hanging on his every word.

The owner smiled at him. She was a foreign looking black woman and Marshall guessed that was why his sister had chosen her. She was efficient and cheap.

Two hallowed words in their family.

The owner let him know she'd get his niece ready to leave. She'd been doing finger painting and needed to wash her hands. He was glad the owner would do it since he had no interest. But to his surprise the owner called out, "Joshua, Marie's ready to leave," then went to another room. The serious looking kid said, "Take a seat, she'll be ready in a minute," then took his niece over to the sink.

Marshall pushed aside a black backpack and sat down at a table in the corner. He glanced at his watch then noticed a bunch of papers on the table. He was about to look away when he saw something that made his mouth grow dry. He saw something that could set him free. An idea for recycling fabrics. He quickly scanned through every page.

"Okay, she's ready."

Marshall glanced up and saw the serious looking kid standing with Marie. The kid was foreign looking, like his mother, and spoke English without an accent like she did, but there was still something unsettling about him up close. He seemed older than he appeared and looked as if he could spout a hundred mathematical theorems by memory. If Marshall hadn't been desperate he would have thanked him and hurried out as he usually did. Instead he stayed seated and pointed to the papers. "What's this?"

"A project to help the environment," the kid said.

Marie grabbed his arm and he winced when he felt her damp hands against his skin. "Uncle, I'm ready to go."

"Just give me a minute."

"But I—"

He dug in his pocket and gave her a bag of Skittles. His sister didn't like him giving her sweets, Marie was on the chubby side, but candies, cookies and a chocolate bar or two, were his secret weapon. He'd planned on giving it to her in the car. It kept her quiet. Otherwise she'd tell him every detail of her day and bore him to tears, but he'd sacrifice his silence for this opportunity. "Eat this quietly in the corner. Okay?"

Her eyes lit up and she nodded with joy before she cautiously glanced around, in case anyone else saw her (his niece didn't like to share) before she took her sacred stash to the corner and tucked in.

Marshall turned his attention back to the serious kid. "Is this for school?"

"Yes, I have to present it in class."

They didn't go to the same school and the kid looked like a freshman so no one would know if there was an overlap. "Are you nervous?"

"A little."

"You can practice on me."

He hesitated. "But I have to watch the kids."

Marshall nodded. "Right of course. I only wanted to help you. I could look at what you have and give you some pointers."

The kid folded his arms. "Really? Why would you do that for me?"

Marshall silently swore. Did the serious kid have to be skeptical too? He'd have to charm him.

He flashed his most engaging grin, the one that had gotten Latasha to forgive him for standing her up twice and convinced his Chemistry teacher to shift his D to a C through extra credits. "That's just the kind of guy I am, but if you don't want my help I understand."

The kid looked at him for a long time before he said, "Sure. Tell me what you think."

Marshall seized on the papers like a scavenger digging for gold. The kid's research was impeccable, the idea amazing. He spent several minutes taking notes. He had never taken so many notes in his life. And what he couldn't write down he memorized. He could replicate anything visual like pie charts and graphs and diagrams like a forger, without understanding a thing.

This kid didn't know what he had and with some improvements this was the kind of project that would get him the A he needed. He gave the kid some cursory advice before he left and then worked all night finishing his paper.

He got a C for his efforts, but he didn't care. At least he hadn't come up with nothing and he got some points for creativity. However, the average grade had dampened some enthusiasm for the project and he started seeing it with a more jaundiced eye.

He was stupid to think that some kid knew about the realities of business. How could he have thought his project would have done better?

Marshall tucked the project away, but it made its way back into his life while in graduate school.

He'd been clearing up his apartment after a bad breakup, wanting to torch any image he could find of the girl who'd broken his heart, and desperate for inspiration for the capstone project proposal he had to hand in to his professor. He had barely a week left to finish and submit it. The final project was to represent all that he'd learned so far while in graduate school and would dictate the direction of his next two semesters. He toyed with the idea of dropping out of school and saving himself the misery when he saw the paper again, tucked inside an accounting book.

He didn't care about reusing the idea; he wasn't into school. He knew that he just needed an MS degree to please his father and then he'd be welcomed into the business so his future was set. But he didn't know how to make the paper college level ready so he went to the library hoping to figure out a way to expand it so it didn't look like he'd stolen some high school kid's homework.

That's where he met her.

"Are you all right?" a woman said.

He didn't know how long he'd been sitting alone at the table scouring the stack of books in front of him, hoping by magic everything would make sense. But when he looked up there were fewer people in the library and the sun had disappeared.

He looked up at the woman, wondering why she seemed vaguely familiar. He had a sense he knew her from somewhere but couldn't place her. Not that that was a surprise. She was cute but not much of a looker. She wore a quirky, but stylish top and jeans. A design student, maybe? He saw concern in her brown gaze and he was too sad and tired to lie. "No, I'm not all right. I've got to work on a proposal for my professor and I can't put together all that I've learned into one simple idea."

She pulled out a chair. "Mind if I helped?"

He shrugged. He didn't care. He didn't see any way out of this. He already knew he wasn't as smart as his father and he'd never be a success like him. Plus, he didn't see how a C project could help him now. "Sure." He held out his hand. "Marshall."

She smiled. "I know. We took *Budget Formulation* together."

Ah...yes. She'd been in one of his boring classes. That's where he remembered her from. Too bad he didn't remember her name. But she didn't offer it, instead she started reading over his work.

He pretended to do the same, but covertly played a game on his phone waiting for her to finish.

"You came up with this?" the woman finally said with awe in her voice.

It was her awe that surprised him. He looked up at her. "Uh...yeah."

"It's incredible."

He didn't see what was so incredible about a project that had gotten him a C even when she helped him sketch out his introduction and theories. He didn't understand half of what she said. But he saw her enthusiasm and knew he could use that to his advantage. He wasn't surprised when she quickly said 'yes' when he suggested they should submit the proposal as a team since they shared the same professor. He wasn't surprised that over the next two semesters she didn't mind doing all the heavy lifting for their project as long as he told her he was impressed. A woman like Karen lived on compliments and Marshall could flatter the mane off a lion.

But she turned their project into something more—something beyond the solid B that they got. She turned it into a business.

"I'm not great with ideas, but I know how to make things happen," she told him when she encouraged him to form a professional business and he agreed to partner with her. That was no lie. To him she spun wheat into gold. Before he knew it he was the CEO of a booming business that steadily continued to grow. His father was impressed and complimented him about having the family genes.

Seven years later he should be happy. But he was scared because that serious, foreign looking kid had grown up into a man and that man hadn't said anything. Probably didn't even recognize Marshall. But Marshall recognized him. Akibu had a manner and dark, penetrating gaze one didn't forget. Marshall kept waiting for him to storm into his office and accuse him of stealing his idea.

He was ready for a lawsuit. Successful people always faced such possibilities. He wasn't worried about that. He kept his lawyers well informed. He knew his argument. You can't copyright ideas. There was no proof. There were plenty of kids who'd come up with ideas. He wasn't the first to think of it. He expected a fight.

It's what he didn't expect that truly bothered him. Akibu did nothing. Absolutely nothing.

Nothing at all.

Except try to undermine him. Slowly, patiently.

That's why he wanted—no needed—him gone. He asked their employees how they felt around him and most didn't have much of an opinion except for one guy who had a distinct dislike for anybody with a pulse. They only kept him because he was brilliant and worked from home most times. However, Marshall knew that Akibu's performance review would make dismissing him easy. There were enough areas where Akibu showed marked weakness and no one would know it was personal.

Then Karen had to ruin his perfect plan.

Marshall rubbed a hand over his face. He'd gotten cold sitting in the parked car, but the cold felt good.

Where the hell had a baby come from? And who cared? A guy like Akibu could get another job. But she'd been adamant and now she wanted to completely restructure the performance review process. Where had things gone so wrong? And he hadn't been able to change her mind with flattery and food. It used to always work.

Until now. Until Akibu. Until his damn ideas.

Marshall rubbed his forehead, feeling the tension at his temple.

He had to shake her up before it was too late. Remind her that they needed each other. That she needed him.

He'd made a grave mistake by giving her an ultimatum. He only now realized how arrogant he'd been to force her hand. Having her work with Akibu was a mistake. Those two would be too powerful together. It was better that he keep them apart and behind him.

A leader knew what generals to hire. He had upset her and needed to regain her trust and he needed to keep Akibu close just in case he tried anything. Loyalty had to be his weapon not force. He had to find a way to change her mind, to rattle her to let her start taking him seriously.

CHAPTER 15

She'd never felt so alive.

Karen walked the empty halls of the 3R building feeling revived.

She twirled in the hall. She finally understood why Marshall had gotten bored of her mentioning the past. She no longer had to hold onto him that way. The present and the future were what mattered now. Joshua had shown her that.

He had helped her to break out of a stupor. She'd been so busy managing and making sure Marshall was happy that she'd lost track of what was truly important. What they had built together. Marshall could get lost in the weeds sometimes too. Just as she had before, she had to be strong enough for both of them.

Everybody knows.

Karen felt her face burn at the memory of Joshua's words. She pressed her hands to her cheeks. Had she really been that obvious? She let her hands fall to her sides and sighed. She wouldn't be ashamed of her feelings. It was so nice of Joshua to say Marshall was an idiot for not noticing her. Of course that wasn't true. Marshall was far from an idiot and he didn't notice her because he'd gotten used to her. However, this was her chance. She'd shaken him up today. She could see it in his eyes. She'd continue on this journey and help Joshua see her as she really was.

Marshall. She meant to say Marshall. Why had she said Joshua instead? Karen shook her head. It was getting late and it had been a busy day. Plus she'd had such an interesting conversation with him today, that's why he had been on her mind. It was nothing more than that.

But as Karen walked to her car, for the first time she didn't think of what Marshall was doing or who he was doing it with. Instead she was wondering whether a stuffed teddy bear had made a baby smile.

rank had money.

Frank *never* had money.

The hundred dollar bill was the first sign to Tilly that something was wrong.

"What's going on?" she asked him, staring at the money he held out to her as if it were a dead snake. Looking after Olivia had been easier than she'd imagined. She'd at first thought that having to stay at Joshua's place would have proved a nuisance and suggested she pick up Olivia so she could work from home. But he'd told her he'd taken special care to child proof the place and didn't want the baby to stay anywhere else until he was ready to take her to CPS in January.

She'd had a good day thinking that the extra money she was getting from Joshua was worth it when she'd returned to her apartment to find her brother lounged out on the couch wearing new jeans with a grin and waving money at her.

"What do you mean?" Frank said.

"You know what I mean. First you treat me to dinner and now you're giving me a hundred dollars."

"Because I owe you."

"Answer my question."

"I got another job."

Tilly folded her arms. "Doing what?"

"Why do you have to be so suspicious?"

"Unless you tell me where you got the money I'm not taking it."

"Helped a friend move some stuff, that's all."

"Put it away. It makes me nervous."

"Fine. Your loss. When are you picking Mom up tomorrow?"

"What do you mean..." She pulled out her cell phone and looked at her calendar. She'd scheduled to take her mother to a doctor's appointment? She didn't remember scheduling that. But it was too late to cancel. "Damn! I forgot."

"When are you heading over to Joshua's tomorrow?"

She doubted that Joshua would feel comfortable with her taking Olivia with her to the appointment and she didn't want to have to explain to her mother why she was looking after a baby. She'd ask too many questions like 'Whose baby is it?' 'What friend of yours had a baby?' and so on. "I can't do both." She scrolled for his number to call him. " Maybe I can call him and say—"

Frank took the cell phone from her. "Let me look after Olivia. You look after Mom."

Although it was a logical solution, she still hesitated.

"It's just one day," he said. "What could go wrong?"

Her mother's appointment wouldn't last all day. Just a couple hours and then she could switch with him. He was right, what could go wrong? Joshua's place was very organized and he left instructions. "Make sure—"

"Don't worry. Everything will be fine."

Frank left the apartment whistling.

He didn't feel hurt that Tilly wouldn't take the money. She could be too proud sometimes, but when she didn't have to worry about rent anymore and could relax she would get a little more humble.

It hadn't been a mistake that their mother's appointment overlapped on the same day. He'd adjusted her schedule and called their mother to make sure to remind her in case she forgot. With his sister out of the picture everything was set.

He'd never taken a half-day before but Karen had insisted and Joshua wasn't one to argue with an opportunity. They'd had a productive discussion about their project and he was eager to get to think about the different aspects of what they needed to do.

He knew Tilly would be happy for the reprieve.

The first thing he noticed when he entered his apartment was the silence. Was Tilly taking a nap?

He crept to his bedroom and peeked inside. It was empty.

Had Tilly gone out to run an errand? He'd thought he'd put enough food in the fridge so Tilly wouldn't have to leave. He really preferred she stayed home as much as possible.

He sent her a text. **Where are you?**

With Mom. Didn't Frank tell you?

Why would Frank tell me?

Isn't he there?

No.

Don't worry, I'll call him.

Joshua stared at the text knowing he couldn't do what she asked. He would worry because he had a sneaking suspicion something was very, very wrong.

CHAPTER 17

It was the bright green jacket that first caught Karen's eye. Among the bare brown and white trees and muted grasses it stood out like a spring flower. The park lay empty of visitors who found it too cold to enjoy its expertly designed layout. She'd gone out to get herself coffee at the local cafe and decided to cross through the park as a shortcut to get to back to her office, when she saw the jacket. The design, size and color reminded her of Olivia, but the man hurrying into the park didn't look anything like Joshua.

He was a tall, reed-thin, good looking man but something about the way he kept looking over his shoulder made her sharpen her gaze. Was he in trouble? Did he need help? She saw him stumble and something fell out of the bag slung over his shoulder. When she went to pick it up she saw it was a teddy bear with the name Olivia across it. The exact same bear she'd given to Joshua!

She looked up and didn't see the man. She hurried

along the path frantically looking around for them when she saw the man sitting on a bench. Another larger man sat beside him. She walked up behind the men ready to return the dropped bear when she overheard the bigger man say, "You didn't tell me she had a birthmark."

"It's small. Is that a problem?"

"It may affect the value."

"But I have papers. That should make things easier for you."

Karen darted behind a tree unable to grasp what she'd just heard. She couldn't believe what she was hearing. She was certain the baby was Olivia now. If not for the coat or the bear, then definitely the birthmark on her right temple. Who was this man? What was he doing with her?

"Shifting merchandise is always a risk," the bigger man said.

"There's no worry with this one. She's already been tossed once. Let someone else's trash be your treasure."

"Yes, indeed."

Karen covered her mouth. It couldn't be. He couldn't be selling her?

She had her worst suspicions realized when the larger man handed the skinny man an envelope. She had to do something! She darted out from behind the tree, grabbed the baby and ran.

Which wasn't easy. The baby was heavier than she looked. She puffed her way through the park wishing she'd done more cardio workouts and was near the exit of the park when someone grabbed the collar of her coat and spun her around. She felt his nails bite into her neck.

"What the hell are you doing?" the skinny man said.

"Fire!" She called out but there was no one around to hear her and she was so winded her voice barely came out as a squeak.

He briefly squeezed her throat before he covered her mouth with his hands. "Shut up and I won't hurt you."

Olivia started to cry.

Karen glared at him. She tried to knee him but he moved too quickly. Fortunately, he didn't expect her to head butt him. They both stumbled back from the force of the blow, she briefly seeing stars, but the surprise attack gave her enough time to dart across the street and inside a building. She ducked into the ladies' room and waited a few minutes, as Olivia continued to cry, before she left and dashed to her car. She took a deep breath before she pulled out her cell phone and called her friend and said, "Trisha, I need your help."

CHAPTER 18

Shock turned to anger then fear.

Joshua stood in the middle of his living room unable to believe what he was hearing. "What?"

"I lost her," Frank told him over the phone. "I-I went out for a little walk and some crazy bitch stole her from me. Maybe the mother changed her mind."

"I told Tilly I didn't want her taken out."

"It was just for a couple minutes. I thought it would be good for her."

Joshua took a deep, steadying breath. "What did this woman look like?"

"Crazy."

His voice turned hard. "That is not a helpful description."

"I didn't get a good look at her. She was black, medium height, dark hair."

"Well done. You've successfully excluded a few million people."

"I'm sorry. I didn't think this would happen."

Joshua squeezed his eyes shut. He had to think and be rational. Getting angry at Frank wouldn't help Olivia. "It's not your fault. I'll contact the police—"

Frank's voice rose in panic. "Why would you do that?"

"I can't have a baby snatcher go free. If she's as crazy as you say Olivia might be in danger."

"I don't think so. Maybe this is for the best. You wanted to get rid of her anyway."

"Not like this."

"Don't call the police."

"Where were you?"

"I told you. At the park."

"There may be cameras at the entrance or exit."

Frank's voice cracked. "Cameras?"

"Yes, perhaps the police can get an image and—"

"Don't call the police. You could get in trouble too."

"Why would I get in trouble?"

He stumbled over his words. "B-because the kid's not yours."

"That doesn't matter right now."

"Wait. Don't do anything. I'll be there."

Joshua didn't want to wait for him, but he knew he couldn't be reckless either, although fear gripped him like a vise.

How could this have happened? He didn't want to think of poor Olivia crying and scared. Had she been fed? Had she been changed? Was she cold? Would they hurt her? No, he couldn't think about that. He would find a way to get her back. This was his punishment for using someone's life for his gain. He shouldn't have kept her. He should have dropped her off at a hospital or gone to another police station that wasn't as busy. But now he would do anything to get her back safely. He didn't care what it would cost him.

Someone knocked on the door.

He froze.

Frank had said he was at the park, he didn't know of a park close by. How had he gotten to his apartment so soon? Joshua swung the door open ready to release his anger and frustration no matter how useless it would be, but any angry words died on his lips when he saw Karen.

Karen?

He blinked twice to make sure he wasn't dreaming. When he realized he wasn't, he shook his head. If she wanted to work on the project she was going to be disappointed. "This isn't a good time."

"I know," she said in a gentle voice. "It's okay. She's safe." She held up Olivia's teddy bear.

He stared at the dirty stuffed animal. Why did she have Olivia's teddy bear? "What?"

Karen turned the bear to face her and brushed off some of the dirt and grass. "Sorry, I dropped it. I had to go back and get it later and was so happy it was still there."

She wasn't making any sense. "I don't understand."

"Sit down and I'll tell you. Do you want some tea?"

Joshua closed the door confused. He didn't want to sit down. Why was she acting like he was the guest in his own home? "No."

"You're handling it well, but I know you're upset. You're worried about Olivia, right?"

"Yes," he admitted in a tight voice. "I just got a call from someone I'd hired to look after her." He sighed and shook his head. He didn't know how much to tell her but he had to tell someone. "But he lost sight of her and now I don't know where she is."

"She's with me."

"I'm sorry?"

"This is going to take a lot of explaining. It's a crazy story. I can still hardly believe it myself. I tried to call you, but couldn't get through. I have a trusted friend looking after her so you don't need to worry."

He frowned. "I don't understand."

"Olivia is safe. She's with me." She held up the teddy bear again. "That's why I brought this as proof."

Joshua stood motionless then let the words sink in. Safe. Olivia. Safe. Trusted Friend. Safe. She was safe. Olivia was safe.

The relief that filled him nearly made his legs give way. It was the only thing to explain what he did next. Why he pulled Karen into his arms and hugged her.

Tight.

He wanted to thank her, but his throat closed instead and for a moment he was afraid his emotions would get the better of him. What surprised him more was when he felt her arms encircle him and she hugged him back. "It's going to be okay," she said in a voice that made him believe her and he rarely believed anyone.

Her voice was gentle but her body felt strong, solid. He liked holding her; she fit perfectly in his arms. He briefly closed his eyes as his panic dissipated, taking refuge in the scent of papaya from her shampoo, the soft brush of her cheek against his. It was when she made a small sound that he opened his eyes and realized he was holding her longer than he should have. He silently swore, gathered himself and stepped back. "I'm sorry that—"

She smiled at him. "No need to apologize you must have been in a panic." She took off her jacket. "Now let me make you something—"

The doorbell rang.

"Hold on a minute," Joshua said and opened the door.

Frank burst into the room. "This crazy woman just—"

When Frank and Karen saw each other they both said in horror, "You!"

Frank pointed at her. "What is *she* doing here?"

Karen pointed back at him. "What is *he* doing here?"

"You better watch out for knives."

"Shut up, Frank," Joshua said.

Karen's eyebrows shot up. "Frank? You know this man?"

Frank frantically shook his hands at her. "This is the crazy woman!"

Joshua held up his hands and said in a firm, demanding voice, "One of you needs to stop shouting and tell me what's going on."

"She's the one who stole Olivia," Frank said.

Karen shook her head. "I didn't steal her. I saved her from being sold."

"What?" Joshua said.

Frank laughed. "I told you she was crazy."

"I'm not crazy," Karen said. "I was in the park. I overheard you talking to that man."

Joshua pinched the bridge of his nose as if in pain. He motioned to the kitchen with a jerk of his head. "Frank, explain."

"You don't believe me?" Karen said.

"I'll get to you in a minute," Joshua said. "If you don't mind waiting here, Frank and I need to clarify a few things first."

"He'll lie."

Joshua sent her a look that promised he'd uncover the truth. "Don't worry. I'll be right back." He grabbed Frank's arm and dragged him into the kitchen before he switched to a pidgin English they'd used mostly as children that borrowed words from French and Yoruba. They could both speak it at a pace so fast that it wouldn't sound like English at all and make it hard for Karen to understand them. "Start talking."

"She doesn't know what she's saying."

"Tilly told me about the money."

"When?"

"When she told me that you were supposed to be looking after Olivia. When she told me that she tried to call you, but you didn't call her back. When I called her back after you didn't reply to any of my texts about where you were. That's when."

Frank hung his head.

"What have you done?"

Frank took a deep breath before he said in a rush, "I promised this guy I could get him a baby."

"And where were you going to get this baby?"

He motioned towards Joshua.

"From me?"

He nodded.

"Without telling me?"

He nodded again.

"Why did you do that?"

"The money's good," he mumbled.

"You'll have to give it back."

Frank rubbed his left arm. "I already spent most of it. I was supposed to get the remainder of the payment today, but the guy took it back."

Joshua swore.

"Nobody wanted her. You didn't want to keep her, right? You said so yourself. You barely could stand the thought of looking after her for three weeks. I saw an opportunity."

Joshua grabbed his collar, wanting to squeeze some sense into him, and said in a cold voice, "An opportunity? You see a helpless infant and you see an opportunity?"

"It would have worked out."

Joshua released Frank's collar in disgust and wiped his hands together as if he'd just hauled out trash. "You're the reason people don't trust Nigerians."

Frank sniffed without remorse. "As if you're any better. Are you going to tell her that the kid isn't yours? That's just a different kind of fraud, isn't it?"

"I'm not doing it for profit."

"You're doing it to save your job."

"It's not the same."

He rubbed his hands together suddenly eager. "I can

still make this work. The guy was spooked, but I have his contact and—"

"Get out."

Frank switched to Standard English, which was the language he used most when he wanted to get out of trouble. "You have to listen to me. If I don't fix this it will really put me in a lot of trouble."

"You should have thought of that before."

"They're going to want her. They may come looking."

Joshua walked him to the front door. "Get out."

Frank pressed his hands together. "Please."

"Talk to you later." Joshua shoved him outside and closed the door then turned and saw Karen. He briefly swore. She'd been so quiet he'd forgotten she was there.

"Pack your things," she said.

"What?"

"I overheard what that man said before he left. Was he threatening you?"

"No."

"But he said they will look for her. I may not have understood the rest, but I understood that. You can't stay here. He might come back."

"It's not—"

"You go pack and I'll gather the rest of Olivia's things. I'm not taking 'no' for an answer."

From the look on her face and her tone he knew there was no point in arguing with her. He quickly grabbed an overnight bag then met her in the living room.

"You hardly have any stuff for her," Karen said

surprised. "I only found extra diapers and wipes. If you have—"

"It's been a stressful time," he cut in. "I only got her recently." Not a complete lie.

"I bet. It's okay." She flashed a smile of encouragement. "You've got someone on your side now."

CHAPTER 19

Wrapped in velvet.

That's how it had felt being in Joshua's arms. Like being wrapped in a velvet dress accented with ribbons of chocolate silk. The sensation had surprised Karen. He smelled good too like sweetened hazelnuts and baby powder. She hadn't expected him to hug her. Such an unexpected show of emotion should have felt strange or awkward but instead it felt right. Good. Delicious.

No, that was wrong. She didn't know where that wayward thought had sprung from.

She stole a glance at him as he sat in the passenger seat of her Honda Accord hybrid. He didn't say anything.

She'd been surprised by how sparse and masculine his apartment was. No pictures of Olivia anywhere, no toys or extra baby blankets. She saw a portable baby cot but not a proper crib. Had Olivia's mother taken everything out of spite or had they struggled and he'd finally gotten custody of her? She knew it wasn't her place to pry but she was curious how he'd ended up in that situation. She knew he wasn't struggling financially so what other reason could there be that he had so few items for a baby?

But what she did know was how devoted he was to her. Karen bit back a smile. It had felt so good to be the one to take the panicked terror off his face. Unfortunately, he was a lot more trusting than she'd taken him for. She couldn't believe someone had conned him like that.

She sent him a look, unnerved by his silence. "I can't begin to believe how awful this must be for you."

"You really don't have to do this."

"Yes, I do. I have a spare room. But you have to be more careful. There are terrible opportunists out there. When my mom was in England babies were being snatched from their prams left and right. Gran kept a close eye out. How do you know this man? Did he answer an ad or something?"

"We grew up together."

"I'm sorry?"

He scratched his chin and spoke with reluctance. "It's not that bad. He's my cousin."

"But I overheard him threaten you. For the next few days you'll stay with me. Does your lease allow you to change the locks?"

"Yes, but—"

"Great! I'm going to get your apartment locks and pass code changed. You can't trust a man like that won't try again."

"He won't."

"I understand you have to defend him because he's family but you can't deny that, if I'm reading the situation correctly, he wants to sell Olivia."

"Yes, he did but now—"

Karen gripped the steering wheel with renewed anger. "No, don't stand up for him. It's an outrage that he'd use your kindness against you like that. It's happened to me too. I learned my lesson."

"You don't understand. I'm not—"

"You're a good father. We all can make bad choices when it comes to who we trust. Please don't feel bad about this. Everything will work out. I can even help you get a certified caregiver so that nothing like this ever happens again. Everything will be okay."

CHAPTER 20

The moment Karen opened the front door to her townhouse she and Joshua were greeted by the sound of wails.

An attractive, harried looking woman met them in the foyer with a crying Olivia. "I'm sorry," she said her voice near the breaking point of fatigue, "I've changed her, fed her, sang to her but she won't calm down."

"Poor thing," Karen said. "She misses her daddy. But he's here."

The woman quickly handed Olivia to Joshua. The rush of relief he felt when he dropped his bag and held her in his arms shocked and nearly overpowered him.

His heart continued to race and his hands trembled even though he knew she was safe. The memory of Frank's words still turned his heart cold. *I lost her.*

Only a few moments ago his world had gone cold and grey; he thought of nothing else but finding her. Rescuing her. Making sure she was safe.

He looked over her tear stained face, then her arms and legs, to make sure that she wasn't injured or scratched anywhere. When he was certain she was okay, he tenderly kissed her on the forehead and pressed her chubby cheek to his and whispered her name. It took him a few moments to realize that the room had become eerily silent. Olivia had stopped crying, her nose red but she'd stopped crying. He hadn't even noticed. He looked around and saw Karen and the other woman looking at him with tears in their eyes.

"You must have been so worried," Karen sniffed, wiping away a tear.

"Uh, yeah," Joshua said feeling suddenly shy. He'd let his emotions get the best of him. He wasn't usually like that.

"You must be exhausted." She reached for his bag. "I'll show you where you will stay."

He held out his free hand. "I'll take it and you can show me the way."

"It's okay, you're already carrying Olivia."

"I can carry that too."

"Let me help you."

"You already helped me."

"Don't pretend that you don't want to hold Olivia close with both hands. Follow me."

Joshua tried not to laugh as he watched Karen struggle to take his overnight bag up the stairs. Twice she nearly fell over, but quickly steadied herself.

"What did you pack in here?" she grumbled.

He honestly couldn't remember, he'd been too overwhelmed by what Frank had told him and Karen's demand that he'd shoved whatever was closest to him. "Books probably."

"You know there are digitized versions, right?"

He nodded. "Heard a rumor about that."

She set the bag down once they reached the top of the stairs. He nudged her aside and grabbed it. "Just show me the room."

She stared at him stunned for a moment, looked at the bag with a wary determination before she thought better of arguing and headed down the hall.

She opened the first door to the right and waited.

He walked inside and swore. It wasn't the muted butter yellow room and twin sized bed that shocked him or the sight of the desk with five wooden figurines of dancing bears that let him know she'd given him her office. It was the crib.

She'd bought a crib.

Things were getting worse by the minute. He didn't expect her to go through this expense.

"Did you assemble this yourself?" he asked hoping she'd say no.

"Paid for assembly," she said.

"How much did it cost?"

"My pride."

He sent her a look. "Really."

"I'll take it out of your next cheque."

"Good."

She frowned. "That was a joke."

He set his bag down on the bed. "It better not be."

"You're overtired." She dramatically dropped her voice to a stage whisper and said, "We'll talk later."

Joshua watched her cautiously back out of the room. "Why are you whispering?"

She pointed to Olivia. He glanced down and saw she was fast asleep, her face pressed against his chest.

"'Night," Karen mouthed before she closed the door.

Joshua placed Olivia gently down in the crib then sat down hard on the bed. He briefly froze when it squeaked, afraid the sound would wake her. He stared at the crib ready to jump into action, but Olivia only turned her head and pursed her lips. He released a sigh and slowly leaned back and gazed at the ceiling. He couldn't believe the mess Frank had gotten him into.

You're a fraud as much as me. His cousin's words hurt because they were true.

CHAPTER 21

She felt like a hero. Karen raised her hands above her head as if she were a superhero accepting applause. Reuniting Joshua with his daughter was one of the top three best things she'd ever experienced (second to that hug he'd given her, but she wouldn't think about that now).

Karen quickly let her hands fall when she saw her friend, Trisha Watts, waiting for her at the bottom of the stairs.

Dressed in smart burgundy trousers and a yellow blouse she made business casual look like an expensive trend. But as a real estate agent she always made sure to look her best. She lifted a well arched brow and said, "You know that guy is scary sexy, right?"

Karen walked past her. "No, I didn't notice."

"I did. Is he single?"

"He's coming out—"

"He's gay?"

"Of a bad breakup," Karen finished.

She rubbed her hands together in delight. "Oh, perfect. He'll need comforting."

"Right now his priority is his daughter."

"She doesn't take that much attention."

"You could hardly manage a couple hours."

Trisha smoothed back her curly black hair. "It was an off day."

Karen walked into her living room and sat on the couch, adjusting the poinsettia shaped pillow she'd bought out for the holidays. "Give the man time."

Trisha took a seat in front of her. "Of course I won't even try if you're interested."

"Why would I be interested?"

Trisha slapped her forehead. "Oh I forgot. You're still in love with the man who only sees you as his golden goose."

"That's not funny."

"I wasn't trying to be funny. Give up on Marshall."

"No, this is my year." Karen leaned forward, eager to share. "You should have seen the way he looked at me a couple of days ago." Just the thought made her smile. "He was impressed."

Trisha folded her arms. "Really?"

"Yes, I stood up to him and even made him take me more serious in meetings."

"Really?"

"Yes." She frowned. "Don't sound so shocked."

"That doesn't sound like you."

Karen clasped her hands together pleased. "That's exactly what *he* said. And when Joshua told me that I should listen to how he talks to me, I took his advice. Even made some money." She told her about the piggybank.

"So you did this because Joshua asked you to?"

"Well...it was a good idea."

Trisha looked intrigued. "What else has Joshua said about Marshall?"

"Nothing else worth repeating. He doesn't truly understand how instrumental Marshall is to the company. He thinks it's all because of me."

Trisha started to grin. "Oooo...Joshua is sexy *and* smart."

"Don't you start."

"I think only you don't recognize how much you've contributed to the success of this business."

"I do, but this challenge will get Marshall to see me in a new way, plus I think we've gotten a little stuck with the business."

Trisha's grin widened. "Should I assume that Joshua is going to help you with that?"

"Yes, of course, but...no don't look at me like that. We *work* together. This is purely business. I still feel guilty that I was about to fire him and didn't know he'd had a baby. This project is important for both of us."

Her friend nodded. "More than you know."

CHAPTER 22

She could almost make him believe in Santa Claus and his elves. As Joshua sat at the dining table finishing his dinner, he tried to keep his gaze from drifting to Karen's living room where a seven foot Christmas tree stood decorated with gold and white ornaments and red ribbons; a lush green garland accented with pine cones and berries was strewn along the mantelpiece. He saw a string of tiny lights draping the window, a starburst shaped mirror, and a bowl of tiny candy canes sitting on the ledge. He couldn't imagine an adult without children going through such lengths. But aside from the decorations and the faint scent of pine what really made him think of a magical elf that treated kids with toys were Karen's smiles.

They were also bright, welcoming and ready to appear. How could someone always be in a good mood? How was that possible?

"Do you want something else?" she said.

It took him a moment to realize she was talking to him. He wasn't used to people caring about what he thought of or asking if he needed anything. He looked down at the plate of chicken stir-fry and yellow rice she'd made. "Um, no this is great." It was better than great. It was something she'd reheated and apologized for but he was used to his frozen dinners and takeaway so a home cooked meal was a great change. Olivia had already eaten and was happily playing on the ground with a crawl-along toy shaped like a hippo. At first he'd been nervous because he knew the trouble Olivia could get into, until he saw that Karen had created a safe place in the living room for her to play in where they could watch her.

"You don't have to worry about going into work tomorrow," Karen said.

"What?"

"I'm going to ask for a week's extension until after the holidays for our presentation so that you can relax."

"But I don't—"

"You're going to telecommute tomorrow. Longer if necessary."

"But—"

Her cell phone buzzed. She glanced down. "Sorry, I have to take this." She stood. "We'll talk more later."

But she didn't give him a chance for later. By the time he woke up the next day, she'd gone but she'd left him a note in the bathroom with a fresh set of towels telling him 'Good morning' and left him a note on the black, concrete kitchen counter telling him what he could heat up and that he didn't have to worry about anything.

Which only made him worry more. She was too kind

and he didn't want to exploit it. He had to deal with Frank first then he'd figure out what to do next.

He called Tilly. "Where's Frank? I can't reach him."

"Where are you?"

"I can't tell you that. Where's Frank?"

"What's he done?"

He paused. She didn't sound surprised that he was looking for her brother. "What do you mean?" She sighed resigned. "Where did the money come from?"

He told her about Olivia. She swore then said, "This is worse than I thought. He didn't come home yesterday. I don't know where he is right now, but he'll surface soon."

"When he does, you let me know."

She hesitated. "Where are you again?"

"I told you I can't say..." He paused. "What's wrong?"

"I'm scared. If they're looking for Frank they may come after me. What if these people are really dangerous? Can I stay at your place?"

"Yes, sure...wait. No, that's not a good idea. Besides she's getting the locks changed and—"

"Who?"

"Doesn't matter. I'm sorry you can't stay at my place for now. I don't think they'll come after you, but stay with your parents, a friend or another relative until I call."

"Thanks."

Joshua disconnected the call and stared at it. He had to find Frank.

Karen blinked not sure she'd heard him correctly. Joshua

had already stayed with her for nearly four days and although she'd had to get used to a stray toy in the hallway, baby bottles on the drying wrack or seeing him intently working on his laptop in the living room, her routine hadn't changed. However, today was different. Today she'd come home from work after a harrowing morning, Marshall kept reminding her how much he did not like her extension request; a stressful afternoon, she still had to find a way to cover the loss for the marketing campaign, to find Joshua holding Olivia and spouting nonsense. She hung up her coat in the closet. "I'm sorry? What did you say?"

"If something happens to me, would you look after her?"

She turned to him. "Why would something happen to you? Where are you going?"

"I have to help a friend."

Her brows shot up. "Not the one who—"

"Yes."

"But he—"

"It's more complicated than that and his actions might hurt others. He's greedy and sometimes foolish, but I don't want to see him dead."

She slammed the closet door closed, making him wince and Olivia scrunch up her face. "You'd prefer to take his place?"

"I doubt it will come to that."

She rested her hands on her hips in defiance. "No, I won't look after her. What do you say to that?"

Joshua nodded resigned and turned. "Fine, someone else will."

Karen grabbed his arm. "Don't be ridiculous. She's all you have in this world. You can't abandon her now."

"Then promise me you'll look after her."

He was keeping something from her. She sensed he knew something that he didn't want to share. She knew that she didn't know much about him or his life, but she feared for him. Why would he ask her to look after Olivia and not his family? Did he not have any family he could turn to? Perhaps that was it. Perhaps he was truly alone. She didn't want him to feel that way. "What do you need to do?"

"Huh?"

"What does your cousin need?"

He shook his head. "Karen—"

"Tell me."

"I can—"

"How much."

"Several thousand. I have the money."

"And if they double it?"

"What?"

"People like this aren't the most honorable. If they double the amount can you cover that too?"

He shook his head as if reading her thoughts. "I'm not taking your money."

"You have to. Otherwise I will charge your cousin with assault." She pulled down her turtleneck and showed him the scratch marks. "He gave me this when he grabbed my throat. The charges may not stick but I'll make life very unpleasant for him. Would you want that?"

Joshua swore and she saw a cold and mean expression come over his features. "You should have told me he did that."

"All that mattered was reuniting you with Olivia."

"You still should have told me." He walked into the living room and placed Olivia down in a bouncing seat, which she happily started to make use of. Karen smiled at the sight, although Joshua hadn't looked too pleased when she'd shown it to him the other night. They were safe here, she didn't want that to change.

"Karen?"

She shifted her gave to him. "What?"

"You have to tell me about things like that," he said in a grave voice.

He looked so serious, she almost started to laugh. She fluttered her eyes to lighten his mood. "Yes, dear," she said but when she saw him wince she realized her mistake. She didn't know Joshua's history with Olivia's mother, but she could imagine it wasn't a good one. "Sorry bad joke." She folded her arms. "Besides, even if I'd told you, would it have made a difference?"

"It will now."

She shook her head. "Where were you going to meet him?"

"There's an abandoned building along the river."

"Okay," she said. "You stay here and I'll—"

He shot her a look. "Don't even think of finishing that sentence."

"I can't let you go alone."

"I need someone to stay here with Olivia. I can handle this myself and I know him. He's not dangerous."

"The people he's dealing with are."

Joshua fell silent for a long moment then said, "Okay."

Karen smiled in triumph. "Good. I'll call Trisha to come over, but first I have to change. I'll be right back."

She dashed up to her room and took off her shoes and quickly stripped out of her blue trousers. She had one leg in her jeans when she heard the soft hum of a car engine roar to life. She raced to the window and watched Joshua drive away.

CHAPTER 23

He'd deal with her anger later. Right now he had to deal with his own. Frank had not only tried to sell Olivia, frightened Tilly but he'd hurt Karen. He'd crossed the line. That had to be dealt with.

He parked Karen's Honda Accord near the back of the abandoned building located in an old warehouse district. In the distance he heard a seagull flying overhead in the hazy purple and pink sky and the sound of the river that curved its way past the dock and around the city. He walked to the front of the looming brick structure where he saw Frank bouncing on his heels, puffs of air coming from his mouth as he breathed. When Frank looked up and saw him, he raced over and said, "Did you bring the money?"

"No, I brought an IOU." When Frank's eyes widened in fear Joshua said, "Of course I brought the money."

"It would have been easier if you'd brought the kid. We—"

Joshua looked across the empty parking lot at the lone black Cadillac parked there. "Stop talking before I decide to punch you."

He walked up to the tinted car. The rear window slowly rolled down and he saw an elegantly dressed black man in a fine silver lace outfit. Joshua noticed a wrapped gift box on the seat beside him and hazard a guess. "Off to a naming ceremony?"

"Yes, my daughter's."

He bowed and held out the package of cash with his both hands in a show of respect. "Congratulations, sir."

The man's face split into a wide smile, pleased by both the show of humility and the money. "Thank you." He tucked the money away.

"There is extra there to keep your distance. But also let your associates know that the police have my wayward friend in their sights so whoever he deals with may be targeted as well." He waited, he knew he lied with ease (to his mother's horror, his father had taught him well) but he was always ready to come up with a countermeasure in case he wasn't readily believed.

The man nodded in understanding. "Then may we never meet again."

"Yes." Joshua saw his reflection become clearer as the man rolled up the darkened window. He nodded once more before he watched the Cadillac drive away.

Frank fell to his knees. "Thank you, cousin. I don't know how to repay you."

"Get up."

He jumped to his feet. "But I will. You tell me what to do and I'll—"

Joshua stopped his cousin's words with a slap across the face. Frank stumbled back. He stared at him alarmed and began to open his mouth in anger. But something in Joshua's eyes made his anger turn to fear. He took a hasty step back and turned ready to run.

"Don't run," Joshua said in a quiet voice.

Frank paused.

"I won't touch you again."

He slowly turned and looked at him wary.

"But you made a lot of mistakes."

"I know and—"

Joshua shook his head and shot him a look of warning.

Frank closed his mouth.

"Do you remember the promise we made to Big Mummy?" She was a respected older woman in their community. "We promised her that we would study hard, be good sons and never hit women."

"I didn't hit her."

Joshua nodded. "That is true. You scratched her."

"I don't remember doing that."

"She does."

"I'm sorry. I was scared. I didn't want to hurt her, really, but to me she was some crazy woman stealing a baby."

"She was planning to press charges. I stopped her."

"I really—"

Joshua held up his hand.

Frank bit his lip and hung his head.

"What good son betrays his family? Deceives those who care about him most?"

He kept his head lowered.

"Money is never a reason to exploit someone else. That is not the son your mother raised."

He sniffed.

"You betrayed us. You betrayed your sister's trust, my own, and worst of all, your father's name."

Tears streamed down Frank's face.

"How can I call you cousin when I can't respect you as a man?"

Frank lifted his head, anguish in his gaze. "I know what I did was wrong. I'll never do something like that again. I just thought... How can I make it up to you?"

Joshua shoved his hands in his coat pocket and sighed. "I don't know."

He wiped his eyes. "I was only trying to help. You had a baby you didn't want and I thought of a solution."

Joshua held out his hand. "Then give me the rest of the money."

Frank hesitated.

"If it really was supposed to help me, shouldn't there be some money you can give me? Or did you spend it all?"

"I invested the rest."

"Invested it?"

He nodded. "There's this guy and he told me he could double the money in a couple months."

"You're trying to con the wrong person."

"I'm not...what are you doing?" he asked when Joshua pulled out his cell phone.

"Telling Mr. A that I want my money back because you're going to pay him instead."

Frank grabbed the cell phone. "Forget it. I'm sorry." He fell to his knees. "Please. What can I do?"

Joshua patted him on the shoulder. "One day I'll let you know."

CHAPTER 24

Of course he'd been lying. Joshua had no intention of calling Mr. A back. Instead, he'd looked at his cell phone to check his messages. He was not surprised to see numerous texts from Karen.

After warning Frank to stay out of trouble (which he doubted he could) and telling him to beg his sister for forgiveness (which he knew he would), Joshua had returned to the Honda to look at the texts.

The beginning ones showed Karen's annoyance (which he'd expected, he'd taken her car after all), then anger (no surprise there, he'd left without her) then fear (she probably didn't want to be stuck with a baby) and finally worry. The worry surprised him. She'd been worried about him before he'd left too. Why should it bother her that much? It was a strange feeling to have someone concerned about him. He quickly skimmed through the rest of the texts then replied and told her everything was fine.

But it wasn't fine. He was still living a lie. Olivia wasn't his daughter.

Instead of returning to Karen's townhouse, Joshua drove to his apartment. What would Karen do if he didn't go back? If he just disappeared? Olivia was safe with her. He wouldn't have to worry about Olivia anymore. He wouldn't have to worry that the people in his life could be a danger to her. Joshua parked the car in front of his apartment building and headed inside as the idea grew more certain in his mind.

He could get another job. Sure, Frank's stupid scheme had taken a large chunk of his savings, but he still had enough money to move to another state and live until he found different employment.

He rode up the elevator. He could lie to Karen and say that he stayed away for Olivia's safety. Then she'd never have to find out the kind of man he truly was. A man who'd used an infant to keep his job. A man who liked her worrying about him a lot more than he should have.

He stepped out of the elevator and headed down the hall. He'd have to polish his lie a bit to make it sound a bit more credible, but overall it sounded good. He'd make it easy for her to pick up her car, by sending her the keys and telling her where he'd left it in the parking lot. He stopped in front of his apartment door and put his key in the lock.

It wouldn't budge. He tried again.

Nothing.

Then he remembered Karen had promised to get his locks changed. He pounded his fist against the door.

Damn she worked fast. He headed down to the front desk and they told him they didn't have the key. He returned to his apartment and stared at the door. He could try to break it down, pick the lock or—" His cell phone buzzed. He looked at the number and sighed. "Hello?"

"Are you okay?" Karen asked. "It's been a while since your last text."

"I-I wanted to get some things from my place."

"I have the new keys and pass code."

Joshua pressed his forehead against the cold, green metal door. Of course she did. He couldn't disappear now.

"Olivia, Daddy's home," Karen called out when she opened the door to him. "Thank goodness you're okay."

Joshua stepped inside the house, annoyed by how pleased he was with the greeting, how much the scent of pine, the big wreath on the door and the woman in the red turtleneck and jeans had briefly made him feel as if he were coming home. He couldn't understand the relief on her face before she disappeared into the living room. Had she really been that worried? He hung up his coat then realized he still had her car keys. That's right. He'd taken her car. She must be anxious about it and too polite to scold him.

He walked into the living room where he found Olivia playing on the floor with her bear and Karen sitting on the floor beside her. Holiday music about a magical snowman filtered through the room from a hidden speaker. Joshua bent down and quickly rubbed a finger against Olivia's cheek in greeting before he held the keys out to Karen. "You don't have to worry. You won't find a scratch."

Karen jumped to her feet and searched his face. "Are you sure?"

He took a step back. "What are you doing?"

"Checking to see if you're lying to me."

He motioned to the door. "You can check for yourself."

She leaned in closer, giving him a whiff of papaya shampoo and sugar cookies. She narrowed her eyes. "I *am* checking." She nodded. "But it looks like you're right. There's not a scratch on you."

"I wasn't talking about me. I was talking about your car." He jangled the keys in front of her face. Olivia lifted up her head intrigued by the sound.

She snatched the keys from him and scowled. "Why would I worry about a scratch on my car when you just went to pay a man who deals in stolen babies?"

Joshua paused for a minute. The way she said it made the situation really sound dangerous. Strange how he'd felt more angry than scared.

"And then you were gone for a long time," she continued.

He blinked, looking at her for a long moment as if she were an image coming into focus. She wasn't smiling, there was nothing fun and light about her. He'd seen that expression on her face before when he'd told her about the marketing campaign. He'd really worried her; he hadn't meant to do that. Marshall did things like that, not him. He never wanted to make her feel that way.

Suddenly, he wanted to disappear for a completely different reason. He wanted to disappear because he didn't like the longing tugging his heart. The desire to fold her in his arms and make promises he'd have no right to. Promises like 'I'd never hurt you' 'I'll never make you worry again'. He let his gaze fall."Had to clear my head."

She rested a light hand on his shoulder. "So everything is fine now?"

"Yes," he lied, ashamed how his voice broke on the word as his heart began to race. Her touch. Why did her touch affect him so much? Why was there a tenderness there that he craved? He lifted his head and met her gaze, and a cold, dark truth gripped him. The danger wasn't out there. It wasn't behind a dark, abandoned building on a cold December day.

It was here. In this house full of warmth and light. It was being with her. He took a step back. He had to get out of there. He had to tell her that he needed to leave, just give him the new keys. "Thanks for your help." He bent down and picked up Olivia. She was the shield he needed. "But if I could get my ke—"

She held up her hands. "Before you say another word, follow me."

"Karen."

She hurried up the stairs. "Not a peep. You're lucky I forgave you. I could have called the police."

"You shouldn't keep making threats like that." Especially if she knew about his father, which she didn't.

"What are you doing over the holidays?"

"Nothing. Why?"

"Me neither. I briefly make an appearance with my parents then I'm free. I thought you could stay here for a few more days instead of being alone."

"I don't think—" He stopped when she swung his bedroom door open. Sitting on his bed he saw a stack of diapers, baby clothes, toys and a baby carrier.

She beamed at him. "I hope you like them."

"What is wrong with you?"

Her smile fell. "You don't like them?"

"This is too much."

"No, it's not. You asked me to look after her if anything happened to you. I got the feeling you were without family or friends you could trust and from the empty way your apartment looked, you didn't have the time to get all that Olivia needed. I suspect you're dealing with a breakup and then you were nearly fired and then your daughter was nearly taken. I wanted to help. I wanted you to have fewer things to worry about."

He didn't know what to say. She was too kind, too good almost unreal. "What do you want from me?"

"Nothing."

"Nobody's ever this nice without a reason."

He half expected her to protest, but then she looked saddened. "I'm sorry."

Good. Now the truth would come.

"It's guilt."

"Guilt?"

She nodded. "I wanted to help make your life easier so you can concentrate on work. This project we're working on is important to me and I also feel guilty about you."

"Me?"

"You made me realize how out of touch I've been with the staff and even what's been going on inside the business. I'd strayed from my vision and I don't want to do that again. " She gripped her hand into a fist and her eyes filled with determination. "You're right. I'm not giving you all this out of the goodness of my heart. I'm trying to seduce you with kindness because I want you. All of you."

CHAPTER 25

Joshua felt his body grow hot then cold. He didn't move, afraid he'd misheard her. She wanted him? For a moment an image of her wrapped in his sheets, one smooth brown leg showing, as she held a tablet in her hand going over the ingredients of a solvent compound flashed in his mind. He wanted her too, but what about Marshall? "You don't mean that."

"I mean every word. When I saw you at that conference two years ago, I knew you were the man I wanted. You're exactly what 3R needs, what I need."

Joshua nodded, feeling foolish. Of course she didn't want him that way. How could he have thought she saw him as anything but an employee? "Right."

"Especially now," she continued. "But I need to have you focused, not worried about personal matters. I want you. All of you. Your mind, your energy, your drive. Over the next couple weeks I want you focused on this project. I don't want you to think of anything else. I don't want you worried about your baby, I want you worried about mine—3R. I need your help. I need that brilliant mind of yours if I want to achieve my goals. We can show Marshall what we're made of. I want to win him over and force him to see me in a way he'll never forget. To achieve that we'll have to work tirelessly through the holidays."

"You don't want to celebrate? Why is your house decorated like you're ready to host a party?"

She shrugged. "Habit." She folded her arms. "So, now do you understand?"

Joshua looked at the items on the bed. He understood more than he wanted to. "You could have just told me."

"But you feel more relieved now, right? You don't have to worry about a babysitter, because you'd work from here, Olivia has all that she needs and you have a place to stay without distractions." She held out her hand. "So can I count on you?"

I want you. Her words continued to echo in his mind. But she didn't want him. Just his mind. Just what he could do for her so that she could impress Marshall. The thought made his stomach turn, but he didn't want to walk away. He wanted to see her win. If nothing else, he wanted Marshall to see who Karen really was. Perhaps she'd even see it herself. He shook her hand. "Always."

She'd done it. She'd convinced him to stay. Karen breathed a sigh of relief as she skipped down the stairs. She wasn't sure she'd be able to. She had a sense he was eager to leave, although she tried to make sure to be as professional and polite as possible. She tried not to ask a lot of questions about his personal life, although she was curious. She made dinner for him, only the first night, and let him eat on his own the other days, giving him the personal space he needed. But he was still uneasy; she hoped she'd now allayed all his fears. She drove him to his apartment so that he could pick up his car and run errands for himself or Olivia when he wanted to. She didn't want him to feel hampered by her.

She knew what she'd done was unorthodox but it felt right. It felt even more right over the next several days as she worked with Joshua at her dining table, surrounded by papers, tablets, and laptops, hashing out ideas and challenging each other. When he agreed it was easy, but when he didn't he could be a fierce opponent, which she liked. He forced her to think differently. To challenge the status quo.

It was the first time in a long while that she'd felt confident about not following protocol since first grade when she was in Mrs. Queen's class. They'd been assigned to draw a house and Mrs. Queen had set instructions. A house was to be square, the sun a circle, the trees wavy, the road straight, but Karen didn't want to do that. She splashed color everywhere and made her sun wavy because that's what light looked like to her—bright and free and bouncing on things. She remembered her mother showing her how beams hit the water in the lake. She'd been so happy. Until Mrs. Queen saw her work. She gathered everyone around her table.

"Look at this class. Look at what an ugly mess Karen made."

She'd never felt so small. After that public humiliation, one that still hurt all these years later, she followed the rules. Rule breaking was for other stronger people. Leaders like Marshall and thinkers like Joshua. Not her.

To her horror, when she'd handed Joshua a folder with some ideas from her university days, he pulled out that very picture. He gently pulled it free from the back of a report, leaving patches of yellow and green.

"What's this?"

She reached for it. He sat in front of her and it would be easy for him to hand it over so she could ball it up, but he moved it so she couldn't get it. "Nothing," she said hoping to sound flippant. "I should have thrown it away."

He set the picture down in front of him. "Why?"

"Because it's stupid. Something I did in elementary school."

"Very expressive."

"It's an ugly mess."

"No it's not."

"You're being kind. It was supposed to be—" She bit her lip, heat burning her cheeks.

"What?"

"A house on a street. But I wanted to show the sun shining down on everything making it bright."

Joshua pointed. "Is that little triangle the house?"

She looked at him surprised. "Yes."

"And that circle is the street?"

"Yes, but how did you know that?"

"Did your father or mother work in the space industry?"

"My Dad."

Joshua nodded. "That makes sense then. You did this as an aerial view of your neighborhood. The rooftops were like triangles and the street a circle, that's quite advanced for a little kid but also makes sense. You saw your little cul de sac this way and saw the direction of the sun. That's very impressive."

Tears stung her eyes. She couldn't believe he'd seen beauty in the ugly mess. He didn't see a mess at all. And now neither did she. Now all she saw was a different way of looking at things. She wasn't stupid or uncreative. Something she'd believed for years.

"Did I say something wrong?" Joshua said.

Karen blinked back her tears and briefly told him the story of Mrs. Queen. He frowned. "She was blind. I'm glad you kept it. Did you show your parents?"

"No. I felt too ashamed."

"Too bad, they might have explained it to you too."

Karen wasn't so sure. Her mother liked things to have a correct and proper appearance and her father...

After her father had left them, few things he'd said before mattered to her. Even when he returned she only listened to him out of respect.

"How come there are certain hurts we don't grow out of?" she said in a wistful voice.

Joshua shrugged. "Don't know, but this one you can tuck away as a mean teacher who didn't know what she was looking at. You're beyond her. You have your own business."

"The ideas were all Marshall's though. I just helped him along."

Joshua shook his head. "Stop doing that."

"What?"

"Giving him all the credit. That kind of humility doesn't suit you. You don't give yourself enough credit."

Karen stared at him surprised. He almost sounded angry, but what was there to be angry about? She laughed. "Flattery will get you everywhere."

His serious gaze made her laughter die away. "Don't do that either. Don't pretend my words don't matter."

Karen licked her lip. She didn't know why she also looked at his. Why she noticed the shape of his mouth or how dark his lashes were or how mesmerizing his eyes could be. And she briefly thought about velvet hugs and the scent of sweetened hazelnuts...

The ringing of her cell phone broke her from his spell. She glanced down at the number. *Marshall.* It wasn't like him to call her after work. "Yes?"

"I have something important I want to ask you."

"Really? What?"

He hesitated. "I can't tell you over the phone." That wasn't like him either. "Are you free tonight?"

She glanced over at Joshua. She'd hoped to share a pizza with him later on, but if it was important... "Sure."

"Great. Meet me at Ciccone's at eight," he said.

He'd always promised to take her to the fancy Italian restaurant. She'd have to dress up to go there, that meant what he had to tell her was out of the ordinary. Special. He'd said it was important. What could it be? She sensed it would be a Friday night she'd never forget.

CHAPTER 26

*M*arshall.

The moment Joshua saw Karen's face light up he knew the call was from Marshall. He didn't know why he suddenly felt acid in his throat. He watched how she lowered her chin, lowered her voice. The soft glow of her skin. He even watched when she disconnected and briefly held the phone to her chest as if it were a treasured object.

He didn't care. Everyone knew Marshall had won her heart. Not that he wanted to claim her heart for himself, or her smiles or the funny little way she blinked quickly when she listened with intent. No, Karen was just his boss.

Not directly of course, but close enough. She was the co-founder of the company he worked for. Off-limits.

"Karen—"

She stood. "I'm sorry I have to cut this short, but I

have to change and meet with Marshall in two hours. He said it was important."

He had to come clean. He had to tell her everything no matter what the cost. He wasn't his father's son. He wouldn't be a liar. A fraud. He wouldn't use others for his own gain. He'd used Olivia to keep his job and exploited Karen's kindness. That had to stop. It would stop. "Speaking of important, I have to tell you something—"

She pushed in her chair. "You can tell me later. Right now I have to find something to wear." She flashed a bright grin. "Great job. We made great progress today." She looked at Olivia who sat in her playpen. "Olivia your daddy's brilliant." She dashed out of the room.

Joshua sighed, cleared up the papers then took Olivia out of her playpen. "I'm going to tell her when she comes down. I can't do this anymore."

When he heard her heels on the landing he went to the foot of the stairs ready to tell her the truth. "I know it's not the right time, but—" The words caught in his throat as he stared up at her. A vision in black. She wore a form fitting black dress and heels. His hungry gaze ate up every sensuous curve of her body, taking in the swell of her hips, the shape of her legs, the beautiful fullness of her chest. He struggled to lift his gaze and saw she wore her hair swept back and gold dangling earrings framed her face. A face he'd seen hundreds of times before, but tonight he saw a beauty with silver eye shadow and red lipstick that took his breath away.

She walked past him and the soft scent of raspberries drifted around him. She grabbed her coat from the closet. "What was that?"

It was stupid to fall for your boss. It was even dumber to fall for a woman who was in love with someone else. "Karen, I can't—I'm not—"

"I'm already running late. We'll talk later." She wiggled her fingers. "Bye Olivia." She shifted her gaze to his. "Wish me luck."

Joshua watched the door close and sighed. She hadn't touched him but his body felt as if it were on fire. What had happened to him? Why had she left him speechless?

Yes, tonight he'd tell her everything and then he'd get out of there.

CHAPTER 27

*I*t felt like a night where anything could happen. Christmas lights twinkled from trees seeming to compete with the stars that darted the night sky; a dusting of snow coated cars and pavements. Marshall had never treated her to dinner with champagne. A single red rose stood in a thin, glass vase on the table. She was already halfway through her spinach ravioli and Marshall had yet to reveal what he'd wanted to ask her.

He could ask her anything.

She clasped her hands together and interrupted his discussion about an upcoming trip to the Caribbean he wanted to take. "I know that's not the reason you asked me here," she said.

"No."

She leaned forward eager to hear his words. "What is it?"

He seemed uncertain which wasn't like him and she swallowed down her excitement.

"I've been thinking about this for a long time. Although Mom's been urging me to settle down," he said with a laugh.

Settle down? Her mouth went dry. Could it be?

"We've been through a lot and I don't know why I've waited so long. I know I should have done this sooner, but I hope it won't make a difference." He put a black ring box on the table.

She lifted it up with trembling hands and opened it to reveal a stunning diamond.

"So what do you say? Do you think Violet will like it?"

For a moment Karen didn't move. Violet? What did Violet have to do with his proposal? Then a sick feeling came over her as she realized that the ring wasn't meant for her. None of this—the flower, champagne, ring--was meant for her. The question he wanted to ask her wasn't 'Will you marry me?, but whether some other woman would.

"I value your opinion," Marshall continued. "If you think I should wait a little longer I will."

He didn't have to do it like this. He didn't need the dinner, the wine. Why had he made it feel so special?

She closed the ring box, fighting back tears. "No, you should ask her."

He took the box and tucked it away inside his jacket. "I thought you would say that."

"But you didn't need—" Her voice shook, she fought to steady it. "You didn't need to bring me here."

Marshall flashed a bright smile. "I wanted to treat you. You said you always wanted to come here. Think of it as an early Christmas present."

She couldn't think of anything right now. The food tasted like paper. She wanted to hide. *Everyone knows how you feel,* isn't that what Joshua had told her? Everyone except the one who mattered—Marshall. Clearly she'd been too good at hiding her feelings from him. Otherwise, he wouldn't have done this to her. He'd be devastated if he knew how much he'd hurt her, how cruel every word he said was. But he didn't know and she'd make sure he never found out.

"I have to go."

He stared at her surprised. "But you usually like to order dessert. I can—"

"Thanks for this and good luck."

She'd barely reached her car before she fell apart.

CHAPTER 28

He didn't know what it was. Whether it was the time (Karen had come home earlier than he'd expected, it was barely ten o'clock), or the sound of her footsteps, (they sounded slow instead of the usual quick pace he'd grown used to). Whatever it was, Joshua left a sleeping Olivia in his bedroom and headed downstairs. The soft glow of Christmas lights lit the dark hallway so he easily made his way to the kitchen where he saw Karen sitting alone at the table, appearing like a silhouette. She had her elbows on the table, held her head in her hands and he knew she was in pain.

It was at that moment that everything became clear. He knew why he'd stayed at 3R when he'd wanted to leave. Why he'd fought to keep his job. He'd done it for her.

He loved her.

Without knowing it, slowly day after day, year after year, he'd fallen for her kindness and smiles, her intelligence and sense of fun. He'd fallen in love with her, which was one of the dumbest things he'd ever done in his life.

He loved her and it hurt.

It hurt to see her in pain and it hurt to know that his love didn't matter. But he couldn't walk away either.

He didn't want to ask her if something was wrong because it clearly was, but he didn't want to pretend that nothing was wrong either. He sighed and crept back a few steps then walked towards the kitchen, making sure his footsteps could be heard, although that wasn't easy with socks on, and turned on the lights. He stopped in the entryway as if he were surprised to see her.

"Oh, you're back early."

She looked worse than he'd expected, her eyes were red rimmed from crying, her once perfectly swept back hair, a mess. She turned to him startled. "I'm sorry. Did I wake you? Is Olivia okay?"

"Yes, she's okay. Everything's fine." He rubbed his chin. "I'm just getting a snack. Want anything?"

She shook her head.

Joshua opened the fridge wondering what he should pretend to take out when he heard her whisper, "I'm a fool."

He closed the fridge and turned to her, the tension in his chest easing. She wanted to talk, that was fine. He could listen. "No, you're not."

"I actually thought Marshall would propose to me tonight," she said in a voice so soft at first he wasn't sure he'd heard her. But by the expression on her face he knew he had and didn't dare ask her to repeat it.

He now understood her hair and clothes. She'd taken extra special care. She'd looked beautiful and Marshall hadn't noticed. He nodded too afraid to say anything.

"He took me to this fabulous restaurant and put a ring box down on the table and I thought, 'This is it. This is finally the moment he realizes how much he needs me. Loves me and...'"

"And?" Joshua pressed when she fell silent. He gripped his hands into fists not sure if that was the right thing to do. She may not want to talk about it. He didn't want to hurt her anymore.

Her voice remained soft. "He wants to marry Violet instead."

Joshua leaned against the counter and frowned. "I don't understand. He wants to be violent?"

"No," Karen said raising her voice. "He wants to marry Violet. They've dated off and on for years."

Joshua shook his head, annoyed that he wasn't following the logic of this conversation. "What does that have to do with dinner?"

"He asked me to dinner to ask me whether he should ask Violet to marry him."

His frown increased. "But shouldn't he know that on his own?"

A soft sad smile touched her lips. "He likes my advice. It doesn't matter now. The fact is he doesn't want to marry me and it's all my fault."

She was going to give him a headache. He couldn't understand her and he wanted to. "How is it your fault?"

"Perhaps if he knew how I really felt he would realize

how perfect we are for each other. I waited too late to catch his attention and now I've lost him."

He didn't know what to say. He didn't know how to comfort her. He thought Marshall was a dick. What guy does what he did? Marshall was too sharp to not realize how Karen felt about him. What he'd done tonight had been cruel, but Joshua knew he couldn't say that. There was a lot he couldn't say.

He turned and opened a cupboard. "I'm going to make some popcorn. Let's find a movie to watch." He turned to her and saw her wipe a tear away and pretended not to notice. "Your choice."

She sniffed, her sad smile still in place. "You might not like my choice."

"I don't care. As long as it's not a prison film."

She looked at him surprised. The sadness faded and a new light entered her eyes. "Really?"

"Yes."

"You mean you've never seen *The Birdman of Alcatraz*?"

"Nope."

"*The Count of Monte Cristo*?"

Joshua shook his head. "That's not a prison film. He ends up there, but he gets his revenge."

"*The Shawshank Redemption*?"

"No."

The light in her eyes grew brighter. As much as he was glad to see the sadness gone from her face, he knew that was a bad sign. "But you have to. It's brilliant."

"Two guys in prison."

"It's a story about a friendship."

"I don't care."

"You have to watch it."

"No."

She clasped her hands together in a plea. "Pleaseeee? I've had the worse night ever. This will make me feel better."

He looked at her doubtful. "A movie about prison will make you feel better?"

"I told you it's a story about love. About friendship."

Joshua released a heavy sigh. Although it hurt to pretend his feelings for her weren't real, and it hurt to see her in pain, if he could do one small thing, suffer through one film, to make her happy, he'd endure it.

CHAPTER 29

He nearly cried.

The Shawshank Redemption showed him courage and friendship and love in a way he'd never imagined. He thought of Randall. He thought of their bond and how much he missed him.

Karen cried, but Joshua wasn't sure if it was because of the film or because she was remembering her heartbreaking evening. They sat in the dimly lit living room on the couch with a half empty bowl of popcorn between them.

He was about to ask her if she was okay, when she released a satisfied sigh and said, "Wasn't that amazing?"

"Yes. For a prison movie." He glanced at the image displayed on the parental console for the baby monitor. He saw Olivia still fast asleep.

"How come you don't like prison movies?"

He set the console down on the side table. "Because my father's in one."

"Oh."

He waited for her to ask why, but she made the flat screen go black, turned fully to him and he heard himself talking before he could stop himself. "He's in there for fraud. Not his first time and likely not his last."

"I'm sorry."

He nodded. "Me too."

"My dad left for about a year and then came back and we never talked about it. It's this strange secret that my mom won't let me touch and my father will never bring up."

"My mother can't help but tell me what a mistake marrying my father was. How I'm like him."

"But you're not."

"I try not to be."

"You're not," she said adamant. "You have no idea how often you check the baby monitor. You're a devoted dad. Olivia's lucky to have you."

Joshua bit his lip, embarrassed by her praise. Had he really kept checking the monitor? What was wrong with him? This was his chance to tell her. "Karen—"

"Let's show them."

"What?"

"Your mother, my father, Marshall. Let's show them what we're made of. At first I was sad tonight, but slowly I've gotten angry. I don't want to be taken for granted anymore. I don't want to be a prisoner in my own life. There are so many things I haven't done because I've been afraid. But I don't care anymore.

"I don't care if Marshall wants to buy me out or take more shares. If he wants to run 3R on his own, so what?

You've got so many great ideas. What if we do something together? I can make it happen. That's what I'm good at. I can help you grow a business, a legacy that you can leave to Olivia."

"Karen—"

She waved her hands, stopping his words. Her tone grew insistent. "Hear me out. We would be equals. We'd come up with something that's not in competition with 3R. There are so many areas we can explore. We can be free to do what we want. I've always been interested in exploring a new material for rainwear like coats, boots and hats. I already have an idea of fabric that might work with some alteration. What do you think?"

"Sounds good, but—"

"Great! With a business of our own you'd never have to worry about being fired, or pleasing someone like Marshall. What do you say? We'll draw up a contract, I know of a great lawyer and—"

He sighed.

"You're probably worried about the time it will take to get established and resources. I understand. You have a daughter to support and you just had to spend money to protect her and a family member. I'm not a rich woman, but I have investments and Marshall's offer to buy me out was generous so we'd have enough funds for at least a year. And—"

"We'd be equals?"

"Completely," she said. "I've done this before. I know the market, so you wouldn't be taking a huge risk."

"Why me? Why now?"

She bit her lip and nervously toyed with an earring,

facing his probing, dark gaze, heightening her awareness of him, but not frightening her. It was a good question and she hesitated telling him the truth, but knew he deserved it. "I'm sick of being a coward. All these years I've been waiting. Waiting for Marshall to see me and tell me how great I am."

"You don't need anyone to tell you that," he said in a deep voice that felt oddly intimate. "It's already true."

She smiled, but he didn't smile back. He wasn't a man who smiled easily like Marshall did, but he always made her feel good. She knew he would make a great partner. "The way you say things almost makes me believe them."

"Why almost?"

She shifted her gaze to the window, she wanted to convince him how well they would work together but didn't want to deceive him. "Because I don't believe it myself yet and I'm not sure if you're saying these things because you pity me right now and—"

"Karen."

She swallowed before looking at him again, suddenly feeling vulnerable. She'd shared too much, she didn't want him to ask her any more questions, but she didn't want him to turn her down either. She'd had enough rejection tonight. She needed Joshua to believe in her. "What?"

"Yes."

She paused. "Yes, what?"

The shadow of a smile touched his lips. "Yes, I want to be equal partners with you. Yes, I want to start a business with you. But I also want something else."

She searched his dark eyes, suddenly breathless; her whole body filled with anticipation. "What's that?"

"I want to do something that might jeopardize everything."

This time she didn't ask him what it was, the smoldering look in his gaze kept her still and she didn't have to wait long for him to tell her.

"I want to kiss you."

She stirred uneasily in her seat unsure she'd heard him correctly. Surprised how much she hoped she had. Shocked by how her gaze dropped to his lips and imagined his mouth on hers. But she didn't move. She didn't dare hope that he was serious. She didn't need his pity; she smiled hoping to make a joke of it. "Then let's consider it sealing the deal and—"

Joshua stole the rest of her words away and wrapped them in a warm velvet kiss.

CHAPTER 30

A deal. That's all this kiss would mean to her Joshua told himself. It was just a fun night. Nothing more.

But when their lips touched...

He didn't want to love her, but the kiss told him how much he did. How much he found the scent of her skin intoxicating, how the taste of her lips made his body ache, how he wanted to feel the touch of her hands all over him. He deepened the kiss, drinking in the sweetness of her lips, waiting for her to push him away while his body ached for more.

He didn't know where the wild impulse came from. He usually had more control. Tonight he was supposed to be telling her the truth. But how could he tell her the truth when she was offering him all he could ever want? A chance to be by her side and watch her soar.

This was wrong. He was glad that she wanted to break

with Marshall. It was wrong to keep a secret like Olivia. But he couldn't turn away, he didn't want to. It felt too good to be the man she turned to. To be the man she trusted, if just for a little while. She was hurting. He didn't care that she was using him as a distraction. Let him be used, worn out. He was used to it. He drew her body closer to his, sliding his hand down the back of her dress. He'd enjoy every moment; he just didn't want her to regret it. Please don't regret this.

Karen pulled away and stared at him wide eyed. "Wow. Velvet lips too."

"What?"

She shook her head. "Never mind."

He stood. He had to go. If he stayed any longer, he'd dig himself deeper. She didn't want to partner with the man he was, but the man she thought he was. A single father. Would she still want to partner with a man who'd lied to her this long? Would she trust him? When the new year came he could still tell her that his girlfriend had taken Olivia back, but Karen was too smart to be that easily fooled in the long run. Perhaps if they created something successful...

She grabbed his hand. "Where are you going?"

His heart pounded. Why was she doing this to him? To both of them? "I'd better stop before I make a mistake."

She slowly rose to her feet but didn't release his hand. "Maybe we're both making a mistake." She threaded her fingers through his.

"Karen, there are things about me—"

She pressed a finger over his lips. "I don't care. I don't

mind mistakes. I get to learn from them." She turned and headed to the stairs.

He knew where she was leading him and he didn't stop her. He didn't want to.

He certainly didn't want to when she walked into her bedroom and began to unzip her dress before letting it fall at her feet. She wore a matching black lace bra and panty set with a tiny green bow. A bow. Like she was a gift he was getting a chance to unwrap. He watched her climb on the bed then lay on her side facing him. "Is something wrong?"

He couldn't move. Yes, something was wrong. His body was burning with desire, aching with need; he was as hard as a walking stick and had only just realized he'd forgotten something important.

"I don't have—" He gestured to his trousers.

"An erection?" She motioned him closer with a teasing grin, that promised a world of naughty pleasures. "That's okay. I can help you with that."

Joshua stepped closer to the bed surprised that the pressure of his erection didn't split open his zipper. "No, I have that. I don't have—"

She sat on her heels and rested a hand on his chest. "You don't have to be nervous."

He released a low growl of frustration. "I'm not nervous." He took off his sweater and tossed it. "And I'm not scared." He took off his jeans and let them join his sweater on the floor before he leaned down and kissed her to make sure she didn't think he was bluffing. She fell back on the bed, wrapping her arms around his neck and pulling her with him. And he kissed her everywhere he could, and felt her body arch against him almost making him forget why he'd stopped in the first place. Almost. He drew back before he made a mistake he could truly regret. He swallowed and stared down at her, his voice deep and raw when he spoke. "I didn't come prepared."

She blinked as if in a daze and for a second he wondered if he'd have to explain his problem to her. Then she shrugged and said, "That's okay." She pulled a condom out of her bra and laughed at the surprise on his face. "I told you, I thought Marshall was going to propose. I was hoping to celebrate."

Marshall. Joshua gritted his teeth. She'd worn this cute little set for him. He let his gaze skim over her body —her legs, her thighs, imagining the liquid heat he'd find between them. He wouldn't let this moment go to waste. Marshall may be in her thoughts, but Marshall wasn't here right now. He'd make sure she didn't think about Marshall right now. He'd fill tonight with memories of him. He wanted to hear his name whispered on her lips.

He slid on the condom before he joined her under the sheets. He drew her into his arms, feeling her warm, bare skin against his. Tonight he'd express everything he felt without uttering a word.

He was a wonderful mistake. A glorious mistake. If only all mistakes could feel so good. Joshua made her forget Marshall, when she didn't think she could. He made her feel attractive. Desirable. Strong.

This could jeopardize everything, the little voice in

her head said. Her heart was still broken, and things were still too new between them to risk complicating it. How could they start an affair and a business partnership at the same time?

But another part of her didn't care. The part that wanted to be bold. Tonight she wouldn't be the woman Marshall had rejected, she'd be the woman Joshua wanted to kiss. Wanted to be with. A woman embarking on a path she set for herself.

And right now that path was paved in velvet. Beautiful, brown velvet with a touch of silk. Her body melted against his. The smooth, warm feel of his flesh felt like nothing else. She'd thought he'd be like organic cotton—soft, durable—instead he was a luxurious fabric, her body responding to every intimate touch of him. But when he gently nipped her ear, she realized he wasn't all smooth soft edges, there was leather and denim there. He was still a man with a past, a person she didn't completely know. A mystery.

A mystery that aroused her passion. A mystery that explored her thighs and teased her nipples with a warm wet tongue. A mystery that made her body tremble with liquid fire. She wrapped her body tighter around him, wanting him in deeper, closer. She wanted the explosive pleasure never to stop.

She closed her eyes as the pain in her heart, mingled with the pleasure of her body.

Marshall didn't matter anymore. Marshall wouldn't hurt her anymore. She'd finally found an equal. She wouldn't embark on this new path alone.

However, when she woke up Saturday morning, she was very alone. The space beside her was cold, the sheets smoothed as if no one had been there. Before she could question what that meant, the scent of coffee drifted towards her. She followed the scent and the sound of something sizzling on the stove. She found Joshua in the kitchen cooking scrambled eggs with Olivia tied to his back wrapped in a colorful West African cloth.

She giggled at the sight. "I don't think I've ever seen a baby tied to man's back before."

"It's simple and convenient and makes the baby feel safe."

She sat at the table. Surprised by how happy she was to see him. Last night had been amazing, but she'd expected some awkwardness or tense silence. Instead, seeing him and Olivia in her kitchen felt the most natural in the world. "You sound like you know from experience."

"I do." He set a plate of fluffy scrambled eggs, sliced tomatoes and toast in front of her.

She grinned. "Hmm, this looks good."

"You're out of tea so I picked up some more," he said, placing a box of PG Tips in front of her.

She froze at the sight. *PG Tips dear, not Tetley,* she could hear her mother say. She hadn't had PG Tips since the day her father left. She vowed never to drink it again.

"Karen, is something wrong?"

She looked up at Joshua's concerned expression and

forced a smile. "No, I just prefer a different brand. Do you still have the receipt? I'll return it."

"I'll do it, what do you want?"

She winked and picked up her fork, determined not to let the memory of her past steal from her joy of being with him. "Careful, if you spoil me, I'll get used to it."

Joshua's mouth curved into a rare smile. "That's my intention."

That night she had an intention of her own. She surprised him by showing up for bed wearing a red robe, a Santa hat and holding a list.

"You've been a very naughty boy," she teased him.

Joshua clasped his hands behind his head and grinned. "Does that mean I'll get coal in my stocking?"

Karen let her robe fall to the floor to reveal the red teddy she wore underneath. "No, there's still time to be a good boy."

He jumped up and grabbed her, making her squeal with delight. "I'll be a good boy next year."

Karen laughed as he placed her on the bed. "That's not how this is supposed to go. You're supposed to—"

He kissed her words away then whispered against her lips. "I'm not a good boy and with you I want to be very naughty." He kissed her again, slowly, deliberately until Karen didn't care whether he wanted to be naughty or nice. His kisses were naughty and the way he made her feel was more than nice.

For the next several days they spent as much time together as they could. They worked through the night to complete the idea they'd present to Marshall (caring more about what the other thought than what Marshall's final verdict would be) then spent the rest of the time enjoying each other. They took Olivia to get a picture taken with Santa Claus, went to see the holiday lights at a local park, and indulged in eating cupcakes with peppermint icing.

One evening, Joshua shocked her when he said he wanted to watch his favorite holiday movie. They'd gotten into the habit of putting Olivia to bed before drinking cocoa and watching a holiday movie. She snuggled up to him curious to see what it was. After the credits rolled she turned to him and said, "*Die Hard* is not a holiday movie."

"It's during the season, right? It's a classic."

"Next time I'm choosing something more traditional." Which she did and they watched *Miracle on 34th Street* while he later chose *Scrooged*. They also sketched out their new business plan and agreed not to tell Marshall anything until the new year.

Karen felt happy and carefree until she looked at the calendar and realized the next day was Christmas.

CHAPTER 31

His holiday elf had become possessed. Since morning Karen had been dusting, vacuuming, and using a green cloth to wipe everything in sight. They'd agreed not to exchange gifts (she'd already given him more than enough) and they'd enjoyed pancakes drizzled with strawberry sauce for breakfast and agreed that the day would be relaxing so he was surprised that after lunch she'd gone a little berserk. Just to tease her he moved the starburst mirror on the far wall to make it a little crooked not sure if she'd notice. She did and straightened it. With Olivia napping he was free to tease her.

"Are you expecting company?" he asked her.

"Of sorts. I'm doing a video conference with my parents." She pulled out one of the side tables and set her laptop on top, then took a chair and placed it in front. She then stepped back and looked up to make sure that it showed only what she wanted it to. The tree in the background, the window decorated with lights.

He moved to touch the mirror. "I don't think they'll notice—"

She slapped his hand away. "They'll notice."

"Your place looks great from any angle."

"Thanks, but I want to look successful and popular."

"Popular?"

"Yes, as if I could host a party at a moments' notice. My parents worry about me. They think I'm too focused on my business to have a social life."

He placed a light kiss on her neck. "You have one now."

She grinned, her skin tingling where his lips had been. "I know, but they don't need to know that yet." She glanced at her watch. "I've got to get dressed."

Minutes later he saw that she'd changed out of her jeans and sweater into a sleek, blue silk blouse and black skirt. She pointed at him as she walked to her laptop. "Not one word."

He closed his mouth and looked on in amusement as she smoothed down her hair, checked her reflection once more then sat down in front of the laptop's camera. "I'm calling them now so be as quiet as you can."

He sucked in his lips then pointed to the kitchen. She nodded in approval.

Karen took a deep breath then beamed with joy when she connected with her parents. A beautiful, coiffured dark-skinned woman, dressed in pearls and a purple blouse appeared besides a brown-skinned man with a grey mustache and boyish features. "Hi!"

"Hi, Merry Christmas darling," her father said.

"You look great," her mother added.

"Thanks. Just came back from an afternoon party and didn't have a chance to change."

She heard Joshua snort and sent him a warning glare.

"And you're doing well?" her mother asked.

"Yes."

Her mother peered closer into the camera. Karen grinned. "Mom, you're too close to the camera again."

"But...Wait...Who is that?"

"Who is what?"

She watched her mother turn to her father and said, "Don't you see him?"

She saw her father frown then her mother pointed to something on the screen.

Karen frowned. "What are you two doing?"

"That man. There's somebody there."

Her heart started to race. How could they know that? She'd cleared every hint of Joshua—a wayward book, a sock, a sweater. "There's nobody—"

"He's right there. Look behind you."

Karen turned and didn't see anything besides a man and his dog walking past her window and lights on the wall and Joshua reflected in her starburst mirror as he ate a sandwich in the dining room.

Joshua! In the mirror!

She'd forgotten about the mirror. And in it he was calmly eating and checking something on his cell phone as if he lived there. Which he did.

She turned back to her parents. "He's a friend."

"A friend you have over for Christmas?"

"Yes, he's traveling through town and—"

"What's his name?" her mother said.

"Let us say hello," her father added.

"He's busy."

"He doesn't look busy to me." Her mother sniffed and Karen turned to see Joshua wipe his mouth with a napkin before taking a long swallow of his drink. She turned back to her parents. Best not to avoid the situation. She'd deal with it head on. "Okay, one minute." She dashed over to him and said in a low voice, "I'm sorry about this but my parents want to say hello." She looked over his sweatshirt and jeans with a critical eye. "You look..." She shook her head. There wasn't enough time to get him changed and shaved. "Never mind. You're just a friend. Okay?"

He nodded.

"Grab a chair and follow me."

They both sat in front of the screen and Joshua waved. "Nice to meet you."

Her mother tilted her head. "What's your name?"

"Joshua Akibu."

"From Ivory Coast?" her father asked.

"No, I was born here."

"But where are you from?"

"Dad," Karen said exasperated. "He said he was born here."

"I mean his name? What's the origin?"

"Doesn't matter," her mother interrupted. "What do you do?"

"I'm a chemical engineer. I work at—"

He stopped when Karen pressed her foot on top of his. He stared at her confused.

"We work in the same industry," Karen said. "That's how we met. It was at a conference two years ago."

Her mother nodded in approval. "That's good."

Karen released a sigh. Her mother had smiled, everything would be fine. In a few more minutes, they'd disconnect and she'd have done her duty for the holiday.

Then she heard a baby crying.

She froze. Why could she hear a baby crying?

"What's that?" her mother asked.

"Sorry, I've got to go," Joshua said. "A pleasure meeting you both." He nodded then left.

"Is that a baby?" her mother asked.

Karen looked frantically around the room to figure out where the sound was coming from then noticed the console for the baby monitor on the couch. She'd placed it there when she'd removed it from the side table and forgotten all about it. Damn.

"Just a minute," she said before she jumped up and grabbed it. She sat in front of the screen again. "Sorry about that." She pushed a button hoping to turn it off, she'd never taken the time to see how it worked, but instead she raised the volume so that they could all hear Joshua saying, "...Mummy will come see you in a minute after she's finished talking with her parents..." She frantically hit another button but it only made the image on the screen zoom. "...they'd fall in love with you..." She found another button and turned it off. Then raised her gaze to the screen on her laptop.

Her parents stared at her wide eyed.

"It's not what you think."

Her mother touched her chest. "Mummy?"

"He calls me Big Mummy sometimes," Karen said, forcing a laugh. "It's sort of a joke." They'd gotten into the habit of playing house where she'd call him 'dad' and he'd call her 'mom' she never imagined anyone would overhear it.

"Is this why we haven't seen you in almost two years? You and this man--"

"No, don't be ridiculous. It's his baby, it's not mine."

"And you've known him for two years?"

"Yes."

"The same two years you've been too busy to see us?" her father said.

Karen released a heavy sigh. "Mom, Dad. It was business."

Her mother looked at her father. "How long will it take us to get there?"

"A couple hours."

"Please don't come. I don't have the space with them here."

"So they're living with you?"

She briefly closed her eyes. Caught. "They're staying briefly over the— It's temporary."

"We'll see you soon," her father said.

"Wait, no. Don't you have plans? Isn't it bad manners to cancel at the last minute?" They always had Christmas dinner at their friend's house.

"Fortunately, they're hosting a party so we won't be missed. We'll tell them we'll be a little late. Don't worry, we only want to meet Joshua and the baby, we won't stay long."

"But—"

"Expect us by eight," her mother said before she disconnected.

Karen buried her face in her hands. She didn't want to see them. She didn't want to pretend.

"I guess the talk didn't go well?"

She glanced up at Joshua who held Olivia. She had a smear of white and red icing on her cheek. She didn't even want to know what he'd been sneaking her. "They're coming."

"Who? The British?"

"Not funny."

"When?"

She groaned. "Today. They'll be here by eight."

"We can be out of here by then."

She jumped to her feet. "No, I don't want you to leave." She bit her lip. "Not yet at least." She'd planned to spend the entire Christmas day with them. She rubbed her hands together. She didn't want to face her parents alone, but she knew she was being unfair to him.

"What do you want to tell them?"

She shook her head, feeling at a loss. "I don't know."

"I think we've taken this mistake as far as it can go."

She shook her head again. "It's not a mistake. I said you were just a friend because I don't want them getting ideas. I don't want them pressuring you. It doesn't have anything to do with how I feel."

He nodded before he said in a quiet voice. "And how do you feel?"

"About what?"

"About us."

She walked up to him, wiped the icing from Olivia's cheek and placed it on his nose. "What do you think?"

"I think it would be less complicated if we left."

That was true, but the thought of them leaving made her feel sad. She wanted this. She wanted this day to be special. She wanted to make memories with them. This was her new life. She wouldn't let her parents take that from her. "I don't mind complicated."

CHAPTER 32

Joshua won her parents over and Olivia even more so. They doted on her as if they were new grandparents.

"I'm really sorry about this," Karen whispered to Joshua as they stood in her living room and watched her father hold Olivia on his lap and her mother wave a stuffed bear at her. "They're acting as if she were mine."

"I don't mind."

She was grateful for that. He'd shaved and changed into dark trousers and a grey sweater, although she hadn't asked him to. Her heart turned over at the sight of him, not only because he looked good but because he was considerate of her feelings. She knew she hadn't been much fun after the video conference with her parents. She fussed over what she would feed them, where they would sit, what she would say. He only nodded and listened. The way he listened made her feel less anxious, less alone. He was someone she could depend on and trust, although she feared she'd lost that ability.

"What's this?" her father asked holding up the parental console.

"It's for the baby monitor," Joshua said. "I'll show you how it works." He walked over to him and Karen folded her arms. He really was an attentive, caring father. It was a trait she wouldn't have expected from him. The Glacier had melted.

Her mother walked over to her and sighed. "Joshua seems like a good man."

"He is a good man. A good father too."

Her mother sighed again as she watched her father bounce Olivia on his knee while Joshua showed him the console. "That's exactly how he was with you. He was so gentle. Such a good father."

Karen folded her arms. She didn't want to reminisce about memories she didn't have. "Hmm."

"He doted on you."

"Too bad that wasn't enough to keep him."

Her mother turned to her. "Not that again."

She shrugged. "You can forget it, but I can't."

"It was years ago."

"Yes."

She nodded towards Joshua. "You'll lose him if you're not careful."

Karen turned sharply to her. Her mother's words piercing deep. Touching her greatest fear. "What?"

"You'll lose a good man like Joshua if you keep your heart locked up the way it is."

"My heart isn't locked, just cautious. It was a hard-won lesson."

"A bitter woman isn't beautiful."

"Neither is an accommodating one."

Her mother's lip curled. "You think you're so smart. But you're not. You can't see what's staring you in the face. You're so focused on why he went away, but did you ever wonder why he came back? Why he's stayed with us? That means something. It means more than the one year he wasn't with us. One day you'll realize the difference."

CHAPTER 33

*H*e couldn't believe she'd said no. No. To him. Marshall Holmes owner of 3R. Violet had turned down his proposal without even an apology. She'd actually laughed when he asked her.

Laughed at him.

"You're not serious," she said when he handed her the box. Her laughter, ringing in his ears, seemed to bounce off the sconce lights and windows of the elegant downtown restaurant with its view of the city. Of course he was serious, did she have any idea how much this ring had cost him? He'd planned everything to perfection. A Christmas day proposal. One they'd remember for years. Her gorgeous brown eyes were supposed to fill with tears of gratitude. She was supposed to rest a hand on her ample chest and gasp in wonder then tell him breathlessly, "Yes." Then he'd show Karen what a smart, savvy man he was. How he wasn't a flighty bachelor, but could be a serious, settled man. Then she'd want to please him all over again.

This wasn't supposed to happen.

"Of course I'm serious," he said.

She rubbed the back of her neck, a curtain of dark hair falling forward. "Did your father put you up to this?"

"Of course not."

"I'm sorry, but it would never work."

"We could make it work."

"If you're really serious about getting married you should ask your business partner."

"Karen?" Marshall bristled at the thought. "No way."

"Why not? She'd say yes in a heartbeat and you work well together."

"She's not my type." He couldn't imagine Karen traveling with him, the thought of her in a string bikini made him shudder. Women like Karen had a body; women like Violet had a figure. A gorgeous figure in a form fitting dress and he knew all the amazing things it could do to him in bed. He couldn't imagine Karen in bed unless she had a laptop and production sheet. She was purely a work colleague. He couldn't see her as anything more.

"It's your loss."

Their lunch ended soon after that. Marshall marched to his car, pushing past a couple holding hands. He'd find someone else. There were plenty of women who would want to wear his ring.

But when he visited his parents for Christmas dinner his father thought differently. "You're an idiot," he said.

He and his father sat alone in his father's wood paneled study while his mother, his sister and her family watched a movie in the family room. They could hear laughter.

He was starting to hate the sound of laughter.

"Why? You think I did it wrong?"

"No, I think you're an idiot."

His father's words hurt. How could he say that? How could he have shared the fiasco at the restaurant and his father say that?

"What was I supposed to do? You suggested it. You told me I needed to settle down. To rattle Karen."

"I didn't think you'd ask Violet."

"Who did you think I'd ask?"

"I thought you'd ask Karen."

Karen again? What was wrong with everyone? He rubbed his eyes before he let his hand fall. "I like Karen. I really do. I respect her, but I couldn't marry her."

"Why not? You need her. I thought you'd had the good sense to see what's staring you right in the face. She's an attractive, smart woman who loves you. You could do worse."

"Loves me?"

"You didn't know?"

"I know she has a huge crush—"

His father hung his head. "Definitely an idiot."

"Dad, I think you've exaggerated things."

His father shot him a look of disappointment. "If you think so, you're blind. Karen's perfect for you."

His father's words rang in his ears. Karen? He'd thought he'd ask Karen? Karen loved him? He thought Karen was attractive? The part about her looks gave him pause and worth considering. His father was very discerning when it came to women. What had he missed?

Karen.

Even Violet thought they made a good couple. He had to admit he was little surprised by how cute she looked in the black dress when she'd shown up at the Italian restaurant. But nothing more. What did they see that he didn't? Sure, he didn't want to lose her, but to marry her? She was too intense, too ambitious. Too smart. She made him nervous most of the times, despite the crush she had on him. He could never see her in another way.

But what if he tried?

After a miserable Christmas and boring Boxing Day, Marshall went to work not expecting his bad mood to change much until New Year's. However, he stopped when he saw Karen in the hallway talking to one of the engineers. She wore a tailored yellow skirt and cream colored blouse. She had a nice figure. How come he hadn't noticed that before? She turned to him, smiled and waved. He smiled back. How come he'd never noticed how her brown eyes lit up when she smiled?

He did like her smiles. And there was something different about her. She glowed. She was radiant.

Karen.

He should marry Karen. He'd been so blind. The solution to everything was standing right in front of him. And she loved him, how simple was that? He watched her finish her conversation then head to her office. He followed her, ready to ask her to lunch when her cell phone rang. When she answered and said, "Yes, Joshua?" he felt his heart grow cold.

He didn't like how she said his name. How attentive her voice became. He overheard her talking about their business project but that didn't matter, they may as well be lovers planning a tryst. He had to put an end to that.

Marrying Karen was the only way he could keep the business and her close. He could kill two birds with one stone. His father was right, he'd been an idiot. But no longer.

She ended her call, turned around and jumped when she saw him.

He held up his hand. "Sorry, didn't mean to scare you."

"It's not like you to just stand there."

She was right, he'd been openly snooping. That was out of character. "How was your holiday?"

"Wonderful. Yours."

Wonderful? She'd never used that word for the holidays before. "I'd like to tell you over lunch at—"

Her gaze drifted away. "Actually I've got a delicious lunch waiting for me. Joshua—" She stopped.

Marshall felt as if the walls of the hallway were closing in on him. "Joshua what?"

"Recommended it."

"A carryout place?"

"Yes."

"What's the name?"

"I forgot."

"I see."

"We'll have lunch another time."

"Of course." He nodded then brushed past, her noticing how good she smelled, determined to make her his.

Karen breathed a sigh of relief as Marshall walked past her. She'd almost told him that Joshua had made lunch (tomato pasta salad) for her and that would have been awkward. No one could know about their living situation (she'd convinced him to stay until New Year's Day then she'd help him find a caretaker for Olivia) or their relationship. But it was strange to have Marshall suddenly paying attention to her. He'd never just asked her out for lunch for no reason before. She hadn't seen him since that awful dinner. Was he hinting for her to ask him about his proposal? Was she supposed to congratulate him?

It was the least she could do. He'd soon have everything he wanted—a gorgeous wife and 3R to himself — and so would she when she and Joshua branched out on their own.

She took a deep breath and knocked on his door.

"Are congratulations in order?" she said when she entered.

He frowned. "Congratulations?"

"Violet."

"Oh right. No."

"You haven't asked her yet?"

"No, she turned me down."

Karen paused somehow not surprised. "I'm sorry."

"My ego's hurt and I didn't feel like being alone."

That's why he'd wanted to have lunch with her. She nodded. "I understand."

"Are you free tonight?"

She hesitated.

"The project?" he guessed.

"Yes...rain check?"

"Sure."

She felt a little guilty lying to him, but she knew it was for the best. He looked sad and her heart ached a little for him. It still beat in memory of how long she'd kept her love for him there. She knew feelings like that couldn't be erased in one week, but she couldn't turn back. Although her traitorous heart was a little glad Violet had turned him down, and a small voice whispered that she might still have a chance with him. She realized she didn't want it. As a new year dawned, a new life dawned too.

His father was wrong. She didn't love him. She'd turned him down twice today. He wasn't used to that. She usually jumped at an opportunity to spend time with him. Was the project that complicated? It was bad enough she'd let Akibu work from home so he couldn't keep an eye on him, but he hadn't managed to keep an eye on her either. Her hours were more erratic than before. Before he could set a clock by her routine. But since she'd started working with Akibu she'd leave mid-day, come in to the office in the afternoon and not stay late as she usually did. However, when she worked on a new idea she could get obsessive about things. Maybe she wanted to impress him. Maybe that's why she was putting in the extra time.

He couldn't focus so he roamed the halls trying to get his thoughts in order. He was walking past the break room when he heard a guy with a thick bushy beard say, "You noticed it too?"

The woman with thin brows said, "Yes, Karen looks like a new woman."

Marshall crept closer to listen.

"And she doesn't stay late like she used to."

"She's definitely seeing somebody."

"Who?"

The pair turned to him startled and it was then that he realized that he'd spoken aloud. Marshall knew it was bad manners to eavesdrop or involve himself in office gossip, but when it came to news about Karen, he didn't care. He shoved his hands into his pockets and walked into the room. He flashed a smile, his practiced 'you can trust me' smile, knowing it would put them at ease. "I'm only asking because I think she's seeing somebody too. I'd encouraged her to expand her social life."

The pair looked relieved by his words. "That's it then," the bearded guy said. He'd forgotten his name, but knew he worked closely with Akibu. "I knew something had changed."

"Do you know who it is?" he asked.

Thin brows grinned. "Whoever he is, he makes her happy."

"Even makes her lunch sometimes."

Marshall raised his brows. "Lunch?"

"Yes, before the holidays I saw this delicious kale and quinoa dish she had and asked where she got it and she told me a friend had made it for her. She wouldn't tell me anything more than that."

Joshua recommended it. That's what she'd told him about her lunch today. It couldn't be that he—Akibu— actually made it for her, right? No way. He wasn't that type. He couldn't be. But he hadn't seen him because Karen had said he needed time to deal with a family emergency. What kind of emergency? He had to find out more.

Joshua looked at his cell phone and smiled at the image of an empty bowl and series of kisses, hearts, and dancing bear emojis' Karen had sent him by text. He was glad she liked the lunch he'd prepared for her. He knew their time together was coming to a close. He would return to his apartment and he also had to decide what he would do about Olivia.

He glanced down as she happily played with her crawl-along toy. His heart squeezed at the thought of putting her into care. He couldn't keep her, could he? He couldn't keep up this lie indefinitely.

Sure you could, another voice said. Karen never needed to find out.

Then you'd be your father's son.

No, he didn't want to be that.

He grabbed a pad of paper and pen. No more secrets, no more lies. He had to tell her how he felt.

The next day, he stuck the note in her lunch bag as she raced out the door. His heart pounded as she blew him a kiss and he knew it wouldn't stop until he heard her reply.

He felt like a spy.

Marshall checked the halls then made his way to the break room and opened the tiny fridge. He wanted to see what Akibu had made for Karen today. He searched through the shelves until he saw a lunch bag with her name on it. He glanced over his shoulder again before he pulled it out. He slowly unzipped it and saw a note tucked between a container of soup and chopped carrots. He recognized the handwriting that spelled her name. Nobody had handwriting like Akibu's. Anger slithered up his neck. The bastard wasn't only making her lunch he was sending her notes as well?

Marshall tucked the note in his pocket then zipped up her lunch bag and returned it to the fridge. He told himself he was taking the note for her own good. Akibu was a threat to both of them. He had to figure out what hold he had on her. He was thinking about her safety. Once he'd read the note he'd find a way to sneak it back so she could find it.

However, when he was alone in his office and unfolded the note and read it, he knew she could never see it.

The feeling of anger he'd felt at the sight of the note turned into rage.

The man really was trying to steal everything from him. Not just his business but Karen too. He saw her usefulness, he knew she was the key to everything. He talked about them working together. Building an empire together.

He talked about his love for her.

But what shocked him most was the baby. He admitted it wasn't his. That he'd found it.

The baby wasn't his!

That was it. That was the ammunition Marshall needed to destroy him. To break Akibu's hold. The baby was the only reason she'd changed towards him, without the kid Akibu had nothing. Marshall could win her back.

But he had to be careful how he used this information. He wouldn't tell her yet. No, first he had to win her back to him.

Marshall read over the passionate words again and started to smile. Fortunately, Akibu had given him the perfect script.

CHAPTER 35

She'd been too busy to thank him for her lunch. She'd had a working lunch with the operations manager, reviewed the production schedule for next year, before having a brief meeting with her lawyer to discuss her options after a possible buyout and starting another business. She groaned when she left her lawyer's office and saw the darkening sky. She glanced at her watch and realized it was past six. The meeting had run longer than she'd anticipated. Ouch, that would cost her, but was worth the money. She quickly sent Joshua a text that she'd be running late and that the meeting with her lawyer had proved informative, before she walked into her office to clear her desk and prepare for the next day.

She was just shutting down her laptop when she heard a light tap on the door. She looked up and saw Marshall.

"You're working late," she said.

He nodded looking sad.

"What is it?" she asked him then regretted it. He'd just gotten his marriage proposal rejected; of course he was feeling low. He always moped a bit after a breakup. "I can't stay long, but would you like to get some coffee?"

He took a deep breath and shook his head. "I can't take it anymore."

"What?" Karen swallowed wondering why he was looking at her that way. Like a man. Like a man who longed for her. Maybe she'd imagined it. She came from behind her desk and pointed to a chair. "Maybe you need to sit down and—"

He walked towards her. "I can't pretend to ignore how I feel about you."

She gasped, shocked. "What?"

He flashed a boyish grin that tugged at her heart. "It surprised me too. I've been blind. I tried to fight it since we work together. I didn't want to risk what we had."

"W-what about Violet? And the others?"

He hesitated before he said, "I was fool. I've done all that I can to push my feelings away...but... I want to be with you. I know what I'm risking by telling you this, but I don't care. I love you. I've loved you for a long time. Maybe from the first moment we met. I don't want you to think that this is a mistake."

She stared at him. Marshall? Was Marshall really here? Was this really happening? Was he really saying this to her? Was he really saying that he loved her, needed her, wanted her? No one had ever said that to her before. Before she could doubt it was true, she felt his arms around her as he pulled her into his embrace, engulfing her in the heady scent of his cologne. He didn't give her a chance to say anything before he crushed his mouth to hers.

Marshall was kissing her.

His lips—his beautiful lips—were on hers, sending her senses spinning. It was all she'd ever dreamed. He loved her? He'd loved her for a long time? Her heart cheered with joy. He'd finally noticed her.

At last...

Joshua stood outside Karen's office door paralyzed, grief and despair knifing his heart into shreds. He'd come to the office to talk to her. When he hadn't heard from her after her usual lunchtime he'd started to worry. Had he said too much? Was she too scared to call him?

His worry grew when she later sent him a text saying she was running late. He wondered if she was avoiding him. He didn't want that. If she wanted him gone, that was fine, but he didn't want to pretend anymore. He bundled Olivia up and drove to the 3R office. "This is it," he told Olivia before he put her on his back and headed into the building. He'd face Karen. He had to find out how she felt about his note. How she felt about him.

Now he knew.

He kept waiting for Karen to pull away. To push Marshall from her and tell him that she loved someone else. That she was *with* someone else. That she was over him. But she didn't. She didn't move. She let him kiss her and...kissed him back.

Joshua turned from the sight and walked aimlessly down the hall.

This couldn't be. Something was wrong. Something must have happened. Maybe...maybe she hadn't seen his note. With renewed hope, Joshua raced to the break room and opened the fridge. When he found her lunch bag, he took it out, opened it and frantically searched inside. She must not have seen it. That would explain everything. But as his hand shifted through the empty containers he found nothing. The note wasn't there.

She'd read it.

Sheer, black anguish swept through him.

He stumbled to one of the chairs and started to sit then remembered he had Olivia on his back. He placed his palms on the cool table and took a deep breath.

He was a mistake. That's all he was to her. Didn't she say she liked making them? That she learned from them? And his love didn't matter. It never had and never would. He'd known she'd loved Marshall for years. He was foolish to think that a couple weeks could change that. That's why she'd sent him a text mentioning her lawyer and saying nothing about his note. She wanted to work with him, he was useful to her that way. Just as he'd been useful to his mother and her daycare.

He returned to Karen's office to see if what he'd seen had been as bad as he thought.

He saw Marshall get down on one knee.

He felt his throat tighten as he saw the joy on her face.

This was who she loved.

This was who she'd always love.

CHAPTER 36

Marry him? Marshall wanted her to marry him?

Karen looked down at him, he really was a beautiful man, and then at the ring he held in his other hand.

The one she'd thought was going to be hers. Now it could be. He hadn't known how she'd felt about him all these years because she'd never told him. He hadn't meant to hurt her that night, he hadn't known his heart.

Now his heart was hers.

Now she could feel the weight of his ring slipping on her finger.

Then why did she keep her hand to her side? Why hadn't she said 'yes' yet?

Marshall frowned. "Karen?"

She'd dreamed of this moment and still loved him, but... Was she accepting this too freely because she'd wanted it so much for so long? "You're only saying this because Violet turned you down—"

Marshall shook his head. "No, I was wrong when I asked her. You've been the only woman I loved. I didn't realize until it was almost too late. When she turned me down I was actually relieved. There's no one else in the world for me, but you."

Yes, yes, those were the words she'd always wanted to hear...why didn't she rush into his arms?

Because of Joshua.

Marshall scrambled to his feet. "What's wrong?"

She rubbed her forehead. Her relationship with Joshua was still so new. What if he didn't want to stay with her long-term? What if it was just a relationship to help him get over a breakup? What if she missed her chance to be with someone who truly cared about her and wanted to stay by her side? "This is all so sudden."

He rested a gentle hand on her shoulder. "I know and I don't want to pressure you."

Even though his touch was light, it felt like a weight. "I'm seeing someone."

He shoved his hands in his pockets. "You weren't seeing someone a couple weeks ago."

"It happened recently."

"Then it can't be serious. He'll understand. A few weeks can't replace years of knowing someone."

Maybe, but somehow she felt as if she'd known Joshua all her life. Being with him had been so easy. She never felt awkward or inferior with him or...

"Karen, I know you need time to breakup with him gently. You have a soft heart. That's the kind of woman you are and that's what I love about you. But don't make me wait too long."

She nodded, not trusting herself to speak.

He kissed her and whispered, "I love you," against her lips and she nodded, surprised she hadn't repeated the same words, although she'd told herself she had thousands of times.

She left her office in a daze.

Marshall was right. How could she throw away years of knowing and loving someone for a few weeks of fun? She grabbed her lunch bag from the break room then paused as she remembered the smile on Joshua's face as he handed her the bag. He was a wonderful man. She didn't want to break up with him.

But Joshua didn't love her. Joshua didn't declare how he wanted to spend his life with her. Marshall did.

She grabbed her things from her office and headed for her car.

But what would she say to Joshua? He'd already had a breakup with his girlfriend. They knew they were only having fun. He'd understand that it wasn't going to be permanent, right? It was better to cut it off now.

And they could still work together. He was as eager about embarking on a new business venture as she was. He could build something for his daughter, create a work schedule that didn't keep him away from her. That would soften the blow, right? They were adults, they'd be mature about this.

But he wasn't there when she got home. He'd left her a note that said, "Something came up had to head home."

What did that mean? Was Olivia okay? Was he?

She quickly texted him and he replied that he was fine and would see her in the office next week. She put her phone away disappointed that she wouldn't get to see them on New Year's Eve.

She sat on her couch wondering why she suddenly felt so alone. Marshall wanted to marry her. Her project with Joshua was going well. The business was successful. Why did she feel like crying? Why did she miss the sight of Olivia crawling across the floor or Joshua grinning at her over his laptop?

Why did the thought of not seeing him and Olivia in the morning make her feel empty?

How come she'd grown so used to them?

She shook her head. It was because they'd spent such a wonderful holiday together. It had been almost magical. She walked into the kitchen and opened the fridge and saw a round glass container with a note saying 'dinner' and another saying 'lunch' which made her smile. He took such good care of her.

She reheated the dish and sat in her kitchen wondering why her eyes stung with tears. The lime chicken was so good.

It made her feel warm inside and it hurt too. She pushed the half eaten food away and sat back.

Then gasp as a realization hit her.

She knew why she felt sad, empty, alone.

She no longer loved Marshall.

She loved Joshua.

Joshua was the reason why everything in the world seemed brighter, why she felt renewed and energetic. He was the reason why the business felt interesting again. He felt like a true partner, someone she could turn to. She felt less stressed, less alone as if she wasn't carrying everything on her shoulders. He made everything seem possible.

And Olivia too. Even though Karen was far from perfect with her, Joshua never made her feel bad. Even when she'd once put Olivia's diaper on wrong, or put her chubby arm in the wrong armhole of her shirt, the baby hadn't fussed and neither had he. They didn't mind her imperfections; they made her feel part of a family. A family that would stand by her.

She had to tell him. She took out her cell phone then stopped. She didn't want to distract him if the emergency was important. She'd tell him when he came into work. No after work.

Turning Marshall down would be a little tricky but he'd understand.

CHAPTER 37

Karen stared at the letter of resignation stunned. This was not how she'd expected to start the new year.

"What do you mean by this?" She shook the letter Joshua had handed to her.

"It's my two weeks' notice."

She stood and closed her office door before returning to her seat. "No, you're doing this wrong. You don't need to resign until another few months. We still haven't finalized our business plan and there are contracts to sign—"

"I know all that."

"Then I don't understand. I thought you liked working here."

He sighed. "Don't make this hard for me."

Hard for him? Did he realize he was breaking her heart? She doesn't see him for days. Doesn't hear a word from him and he comes into her office with a letter of resignation? That fierce look in his eyes? What had she missed? What hadn't he told her?

"Is it because of the project we were going to show Marshall? Do you feel burdened or stressed by it? Do you want me to—"

"No, it's not that."

"Is it Olivia? You said you had an emergency—"

"She's fine." He bit his lip and she saw him grip his hand into a fist. "Considering how I feel I don't think it's right."

How he felt? She came from behind the desk and rested a light hand on his chest, making her voice gentle. Didn't he know that she'd stand up for him? That they were a team. "Has Marshall said something to you again? I will talk to him—"

He winced at her touch as if she'd wounded him and took a step back. "Please don't pretend that it doesn't matter," he said in a deep, raw voice. "It may not matter to you, but it does to me. To be honest, even two weeks is more than I can stand, but I owe you that much."

Owe her? What was supposed to matter? Why was working with her too much to stand? Before she could argue he said, "I've got another opportunity I want to take so it's time for me to go. This is the best for both of us."

He was leaving. She gripped the letter in her hand. He was leaving her. Leaving her without a real explanation just as her father had. She was glad she hadn't told him about her feelings. He didn't feel the same. He would go and live another life without her.

She steeled herself against tears. She hadn't tried to make her father stay and she wouldn't try to make Joshua stay either. If all that she'd done wasn't enough, then nothing was.

"I'm thankful for all that you've done for me," he said.

She nodded feeling as stiff as a wooden doll. His words were so formal and polite one would have thought he wasn't the man who'd kissed her and tasted like peppermint icing; who'd laughed with her over peppermint candy canes. Who'd held her in his arms as if she belonged there. No, this cold distant stranger was a different man. "Sure. Wherever you land they'll be lucky to have you."

He nodded then turned and walked out the door.

She didn't watch him leave. She'd never watch a man walk out of her life again. Instead she shoved his letter in her desk drawer, focused on her laptop screen and pretended that she didn't care. She didn't need him. With Marshall as her husband she wouldn't need to start another business either. They'd get over their differences. She'd find another engineer to replace him. Joshua didn't love her, but there was someone else who did.

Marshall.

Marshall had stood by her. He wouldn't leave her. She had loved him once and could restore those feelings back in her heart again. She'd been foolish to so casually toss her love aside. She'd believed that Joshua truly believed in her and cared about her. But he planned to leave.

She'd let him go.

Marshall almost whooped for joy. Akibu was leaving. He had finally won! But Karen looked so crestfallen as she stood in front of his desk with Akibu's resignation in her hand that he couldn't let his feelings show.

"Did he give a reason?" he asked her.

She shrugged. "Not really. Another opportunity and such."

"Sounds about right. Don't let it bother you. He wasn't a good match for us."

"He was perfect."

He didn't like how she said that statement. How depressed she looked. He smoothed down the new tailored shirt he'd bought. Time to get her focused on what was important. "Have you thought about what I said?"

"What you said?"

He winced. She'd forgotten already? If he hadn't

been so happy he would have been insulted. "My proposal."

"Right," she said in a hollow voice.

"So?" He pressed when she fell silent. "Will you marry me?"

He didn't like how she hesitated; he didn't like how she shifted her gaze from his face to stare at her hands. But he did like when she lifted her gaze and said almost in defiance, "Yes."

"You cannot marry Marshall," Trisha told Karen after work. They sat in the café with two cappuccinos and butter croissants.

"Why not? He wants to marry me and..." She let her words drift away.

"And you love him." When Karen didn't reply, Trisha said, "Right?"

"It doesn't matter."

"Of course it matters. Wait...what's gotten into you? You'd usually fight me more about this. You'd tell me how wonderful Marshall is. How this is what you'd always dreamed of."

She sighed, feeling listless. "I know."

"What's wrong?"

Nothing that she wanted to tell her friend. Trisha didn't know about her relationship with Joshua. She didn't want her to pity her. Why did she seem to fall in love with men who didn't love her back? "I've got to go. I'll call you later."

She didn't remember much else after that. She didn't remember how the diamond ring got on her finger, whether Marshall slid it on or if she'd placed it on herself. She didn't remember if they kissed or hugged. She remembered he whispered something in her ear, but she couldn't recall the words.

She didn't even remember how she got home or ended up standing in the doorway of Joshua's now empty room. She didn't know why she was there. Shouldn't she be calling her mother? She was getting married to Marshall. This was her dream.

Instead she sat on the side of the bed and ran her hand over the soft bedcover; she stared at the crib and wondered if she should send it to his place.

She toyed with the ring on her finger, it really was beautiful. Just as beautiful as when he'd shown it to her the first time.

Where was the feeling of triumph? She pounded her fist against the bed. Damn Joshua for confusing her. He'd stolen this moment from her. Why had he made her care? Selfish bastard.

She told herself she wouldn't let him steal any more time from her, but as she made this promise to herself she lay down on the bed. His scent was still on the pillow.

She was happy, she told herself, as a wave of tears started to build in her eyes.

So very happy. She didn't need him. She'd gotten all that she'd ever wanted. She'd never forgive him for leaving. After all she'd done for him? Why hadn't it been enough? But she didn't care. She buried her face in his pillow and for a moment let her body shake with the weight of her sorrow. She let the tears burn her eyes, the sadness gripping her throat making her sobs silent.

Silent screams.

Silent screams of pain that could find no solace.

She soon fell asleep and when she opened her eyes the evening night cloaked the room in darkness the only light came from the faint lights of the Christmas tree illuminating the hallway, which came on by a timer.

Karen sat up and wiped her face. Joshua and Olivia were gone. Just as she had done when she'd watched her father drive away she would move on. She'd get her life back and never let herself be that vulnerable again. She glanced at the ring on her finger. Even Marshall could leave her one day either through death or for a reason she'd never understand. To her surprise the thought didn't bother her. She felt numb to the possibility. All that mattered was now. He loved her now. She'd accept that.

She stood, making a mental note of the items she would have shipped to Joshua's place. She was angry with the man but the child hadn't done anything to her and these items were meant to be used. She'd write him a note in case he protested. She walked over to the desk and noticed a large yellow writing pad and pen. She lifted it up and started to write then stopped when she saw the imprint of writing. She ran her hand over it. The imprint was deep and there were a lot of words. She frowned and picked up a pencil curious to reveal what had been written. Was this Joshua's listing of possible companies to work for? An idea for one of their competitors? She scratched the pencil over the imprints until the writing became clear.

Karen,

I can't take it anymore. I can't pretend to ignore how I feel.

Wait. She'd heard those words before. She read more and her heart began to pound as she recognized every word.

Every blessed, beautiful, wonderful word.

This was almost the same speech Marshall had said when he proposed to her. What did this mean? Why had Joshua written Marshall's speech? Had he coached Marshall? Why? There had been some changes but it was too similar to be a coincidence. Was her heart just a game to him? He knew how she felt about Marshall. Had he felt so sorry for her that he'd... She stopped when she remembered the look on Joshua's face when she mentioned Marshall's name. He hadn't been angry, he'd been hurt. Why hurt? And Marshall had been very happy to see Joshua leave. Too happy.

She held the writing pad to her chest, feeling breathless.

Don't make this harder for me. She remembered Joshua saying that to her as if she were causing him pain.

Joshua had left her. But for the first time she wouldn't stay silent, she would find out why.

CHAPTER 39

He never imagined her being cruel. Joshua climbed his apartment stairs thinking about Karen's face. She'd been truly surprised by his resignation. She'd expected him to stay. Had he really misjudged her that much? Was he really just another way to make money for her? But it was over. He no longer had to pretend. Today, he'd left Olivia with a caretaker he'd hired. He'd call the case worker by the fifth, hand her over and then start afresh.

He'd live his life the way he'd designed it. A life where no one needed him. No one depended on him. No one shook his heart.

He walked to his apartment then stopped when he saw a slender black woman in a peach overcoat, standing outside the door. He silently swore, when she turned and saw him.

The last person he needed to see today was her. Randall's sister.

"I was in the neighborhood," she said by way of greeting.

He nodded and opened the door.

The caretaker stood when she saw him. He paid her before he picked Olivia up and kissed her on the forehead out of habit. He quickly set her back down after he realized what he'd done.

"I didn't know you had a baby," Melanie said.

"I don't." Olivia would be gone soon and he didn't want to elaborate. "What do you want?"

"I wanted to see you."

He shook his head, feeling tired. "I can't do this today, what do you want?"

"Are you really not going to come to my wedding?"

"Why would you want me there?"

"Because you're family."

"But I'm not family. And I'm sick of you and your parents using me like Randall's substitute—"

She stopped his words with a slap across the face.

He stared at her, his cheek stinging.

Her voice shook when she spoke. "You arrogant, horrible—" She bit her lip and took a deep breath. "How dare you think you could ever replace my brother? That we would even consider you as a...what did you call it? A substitute? Do you know why we've tried to keep in touch with you all these years? Because we love you. We love you as much as Randall did. Yes, when he was dying he asked us to keep you in our lives, because he worried about you. He knew what your mother and father were like, we all did. And we felt sorry for you.

"But we also liked and then loved you so very much.

Don't you remember the holiday trips together? When you'd help me with my algebra homework? When you cheered me up after I'd forgotten the words in my first school play? Do you think my brother and I came to the daycare where you worked because we had nothing better to do? Do you think my parents paid your mother so that you could spend time with us just because we had to?"

His voice cracked. "You paid her?"

Melanie sniffed in disgust. "You think she would have let you visit us otherwise? She wouldn't have let you have a childhood, but we knew you wouldn't complain."

"How much—"

"Doesn't matter," she said with a smile. "My parents happily paid and even told us we either got allowance or had you come and stay with us. There was never any doubt what we would choose every time."

Joshua stared at her stunned. "You gave up your allowance for me?"

"Yes. Why do you think we all wanted you there at my high school graduation? Because it wouldn't have been the same without you. You were family. Weren't you happy then too?"

"Yes, but—"

"Did you think we were lying to you when we told you how much you meant to us?"

He sighed.

"We haven't tried to keep in touch so that you can replace Randall. No one could. Especially you. You're nothing alike. But you don't have to be. I wish my brother would be there at my wedding." Her voice trembled and her eyes filled with tears. "But since one brother can't be, I was hoping another brother could." She wiped away her tears. "But I guess I was wrong." She turned.

"I didn't believe you," he said in a hoarse, raw voice, his heart squeezing with pain.

She looked at him. "What?"

"You and your parents use the word 'love' so easily, I didn't believe you. I didn't believe when you signed your cards with 'love from Melanie' or 'love from the Edwards'. I was afraid to. I thought Randall was the only one who ever could."

She took his hand. "You have no idea how wrong you are." She hugged him.

He stiffened, remembering his mother's touch, Randall's cold fingers, and Karen's rejection before he took a deep breath and hugged her back. He wasn't alone. They'd cared for him all this time.

"I'll go," he said. "I'll go to your wedding."

"Thank you." She glanced down at Olivia. "So what's the story behind her?"

He picked Olivia up and went to the kitchen. It was almost time to feed her. "I'm not sure you'll believe me."

Melanie followed him. "I'm willing to listen." She took a seat.

When he finished telling her, she sat back and shook her head. She stared at Olivia who was now happily fed and curled up in his arms. "There's only one thing to do."

"What?"

"You should adopt her."

"I can't adopt her. She—"

"Why not? You're good with her and she needs you."

She smiled at Olivia. "And I think that you love her." Her grin widened. "Actually I know that you do. And you won't have to raise her on your own. Mom and Dad are retired they could help you and I'll do what I can. I always wanted to be an aunt." She stood. "What I'm trying to say is that you don't have to face this alone. Never have. You always have us." She came around the table and kissed him on the cheek. "Family isn't only biological, you know. Family is also made up of the people you choose to love."

CHAPTER 40

She wasn't wearing his ring.

That was the first thing Marshall noticed when Karen entered his apartment. The call he'd gotten from her had been strange, but not a surprise. He was sure she had a lot of questions about the wedding. He was already prepared to let her know that his mother was better at those sorts of things than he was. He only wanted to show up at the church and get it over with.

But when Karen sat down in his living room on his suede sofa, setting a large canvas bag down beside her, she didn't look like she wanted to discuss wedding plans.

He laughed his concerns away and sat down beside her. "Couldn't stay away, huh?"

"Marshall."

He inwardly cringed. She only used that tone when she was upset about something.

"Look, I know what you're going to say," he said.

"You're upset because I gave you the same ring I was going to give Violet, but we can change it if you want t—"

"I'm not here about the ring," she cut in. "I'm here because I know that you stole Joshua's—"

Fear, dark and terrifying, gripped his heart. "I didn't do anything wrong." He swore. The sneaky bastard had done a counterattack he hadn't planned for. "I knew it. I knew he remembered. What did that bastard say about me? Did he try to say that I stole his idea? That's only his side of the story. Let me tell you my side first. We did all the work. You and I. He can't try to take it away from us. Okay, so I admit that I borrowed the kid's homework and I embellished it. It was years ago and it was a great idea, you thought so too. But ideas are like pennies, right? We implemented it. We put in the blood, sweat and tears and had the resources. It was just another grade to him. I've got lawyers prepared if he's getting ready to sue us."

"I don't know what you're talking about." She opened her canvas bag and held up a blank yellow writing notepad. She flipped a page forward to show a pencil filled image with writing imprinted on it. "I wanted to talk about this note."

He stared at her.

She frowned. "What are you talking about stealing—"

"Borrowing."

"Some kid's homework?"

Marshall licked his lips. He had to think quick. She couldn't find out the truth. It was bad enough taking Akibu's idea, but taking this love confession as his own would make him look bad. "It's nothing."

"Why are your words written on this notepad in Joshua's handwriting?"

He shrugged. "I don't know." He snapped his fingers. "Now I know! I asked him for some ideas since he knew how I felt about you—"

"You don't like him, why would you ask him and why would he help you?"

"Because I was desperate." He stretched his arm along the back of the sofa and brushed his fingers against her neck.

She swatted his hand way with impatience. "Stop lying and tell me the truth."

"I just did."

"So you love me?"

"Yes, of course."

"What was that mistake we made?"

"Mistake?"

"Yes, you told me you didn't want me to think that this was a mistake. What did you mean by that?"

"Exactly what I said."

"But why would you think that?"

He threw up his hands annoyed. "I don't know. I was just baring my heart to you, I wasn't thinking about every word I said. Why are you doing this to me? What does it matter? I love you and you love me and..." His words trailed away when he saw her shaking her head.

"I'm sorry. I'm not being fair. I can't marry you." He heard a soft clink as she placed his ring on the glass coffee table.

He stared at the ring stunned. "Why not? I thought you loved me."

"But I don't love you anymore."

He met her gaze. "You will. He's fed you lies about me. We've been together for years. Think of all that we can do together in the future." He jumped to his feet, grabbed her by the shoulders, lifted her up and shook her. "Don't you see? This is his revenge. He wants this. Didn't he quit? After all you've done for him? He wants you to doubt me. He wants our business to fail because of one desperate action of a teenager. He—"

"Never told me about the homework. If he remembers he never said."

He hesitated before he let her go and sat back down. "That's because he's sneaky."

She narrowed her eyes and sat down as well. "Why didn't *you* tell me? Why did you try to get rid of him?"

"Because of this. Because I didn't want him to come between us."

"He didn't. We started to grow apart long ago. I want different things. I don't want to be the owner of a large company and have many employees like your father. I want to stay small and nimble and serve the people we have the best we can. I want to make a difference in this world and it may not be for decades, but I plan to stay on that journey no matter what."

"What are you saying?"

"I want to branch out on my own."

"But you can't."

"There were two projects we always agreed would be mine. That's all I'll leave with."

Panic swept through him. "But I can't run this business without you."

"Then step down and let me be president."

He stared at her speechless.

"It's the only way I'll stay. I don't think you even like this business if you were honest. You want to do something else. Something sexier, showier and more buzz worthy."

She was right. He hated that.

"You can stay on of course. In a smaller roll, if your pride can take it."

No, his pride couldn't take it. His father would never let him hear the end of it, but he knew he had no other option. He was lost without her.

That's what bothered him most about her. From that day in the library all those years ago she was so strong. Stronger than him. Her love for him had weakened that strength and now without it he had nothing. He didn't want her to think that she was above him, that she could walk all over him.

"Are you going to try to win Akibu back?"

She tucked the legal notepad away. "I don't think that's any of your business."

"We're still partners remember?"

"Not for long."

"But before you try to make him one, I think you should know something about him first."

"How did you get the note Joshua wrote me?"

Marshall flexed his hand. He didn't want to admit how low he'd gone to try to keep her. "Karen, let's—"

"How?"

"I took it from your lunch bag," he grumbled. He folded his arms. "But I was only trying to look out for you. There's something you need to know about him and—"

She draped the canvas bag over her shoulder and stood. "I think you've said enough." She walked to the door. "Think over what I said."

He followed behind her. "It's about his kid. Her name's Olivia, right?"

Karen turned to him startled. "Yes. What about her?"

Marshall smiled. "She isn't his."

She stared at him for a long moment and his heart cheered. He'd got her. She'd underestimated him. But before her could crow with victory a slow smile spread on her face that matched his own. "Yes, I know."

His smile fell. "You know?"

"Of course I know. I read his note, remember?"

Right, he'd forgotten that. Akibu had written everything there. Damn. But if she knew why did she look so calm? "Don't you care? Would you work with a man who deceived you—"

"I've already worked with one." She pressed a finger against his lips and held his gaze. For the first time he saw how sexy and powerful she was. He could imagine her in a string bikini and traveling by his side. It was something he'd realized too late. "Like I said, it's none of your business." She turned and walked out the door.

He'd chosen the wrong day to go shopping. But he'd wanted to get out of the house. His mother had called and complained about the linen set he'd bought her for Christmas (great quality but wrong color, dear), Tilly had called to complain about the new high interest credit card Frank had managed to get, and he'd gotten a text from Karen telling him she wanted to talk. He deleted her message. There was nothing he wanted to discuss.

He had enough on his mind if he was going to adopt Olivia. He knew that wouldn't be easy. He'd gone to the mall—a rarity for him—to find a belated Christmas gift for Melanie and her parents. He'd never meant to hurt them and wanted to atone.

But the crush of people at the mall made him reconsider. It didn't take him long to realize that the mall was hosting an event. He saw a large ten foot poster for an author signing event for a book called *Being Real, Staying*

Real. Then another poster showing the time and date the author would appear. There were also two large screens showing the image of a young attractive black woman telling her audience that they could achieve any goal they set for themselves. Between the two screens was a table and stack of books.

He glanced at the fresh faced woman on the screen, surprised she could offer life advice when she was still so young, but she was attractive enough to sell any message she wanted to. She also seemed vaguely familiar, but Joshua didn't think much about it. Between celebrities and influencers most people looked familiar somehow. He noticed two people in dark suits corralling the large crowd of mostly women into a line. He took that opportunity to weave Olivia's stroller through a gap he found. He'd reached past the bulk of the crowd to the partition that kept the author out of view of the crowd. The author stood talking to another person also wearing a dark suit.

She looked exactly like the image on the poster and on the screen, but there was also something about her that he couldn't place...

She spotted him and her eyes widened. She recognized him. How could she recognize him? He didn't know her. But why did she look so...

His mind flashed back to a bobble head doll of a fairy, one dangling earring, a large scarf, a startled expression, and a woman's simple request...

The bus stop!

She was Olivia's mother.

She was here. He'd thought he'd never find her, never see her again and here she was. Staring at him with—

what was that expression on her face? She was silently pleading with him.

She wanted her daughter back. She realized she'd made a mistake. He felt his heart squeeze with pain. He wanted to grab Olivia and run. He didn't want to give her back. He wanted to keep her. He wanted to raise her. He wanted to see her grow. He had no right. He had no legal claim. She did.

He gripped the handles on the stroller as Olivia's mother hurried over to him.

He felt his heart breaking, with every step that brought her closer. First Karen and now Olivia.

His two loves.

He'd lost them both.

He didn't want to hear what she had to say. Like Karen, she'd made a mistake and he wouldn't fight her.

Before she got close enough he released his hold on the stroller and said, "I'll send you everything, there's no need to say anything," before he turned and pushed his way back through the crowd. If he'd been thinking he would have continued the other way where there were fewer people.

But he didn't think. He couldn't think. It hurt too much.

He'd made it to the exit when he heard a voice over the loudspeaker say, "A little girl in a green jacket and teddy bear with the name 'Olivia' has been found. If you're the parent please come to the service desk."

He paused. Olivia had a green jacket and teddy bear tied to her stroller. It was her favorite toy, which he took with them everywhere.

No, they couldn't be talking about her. She was with her mother now. He pushed open the door and felt a cold wind chill his skin.

The message repeated.

"A little girl in a green jacket and teddy bear with the name 'Olivia' has been found. If you're the parent, please come to the service desk."

Joshua turned and began to run. Even if he was wrong he had to make sure. He wouldn't let her be abandoned again. He ran telling himself it wasn't her; that he'd lost her forever. Then he saw her crying in her stroller. No, not crying, wailing as if her little heart would break.

He ran faster.

He saw the author and one of the people in dark suits talk to the woman at the service desk.

"She's mine," he said, unlatching Olivia from her stroller and lifting her up. He held her close then kissed her wet, tear stained face. "I'm sorry," he told her above her scared, angry screams. "Daddy's sorry. I won't leave you like that again."

"Yes, he's the father," he heard the author say. "I saw them get separated."

He didn't know why she was lying, but he didn't care. Olivia was safe. Loud and angry, but safe.

"You should be more careful," the woman at the service desk scolded him.

He held Olivia tight and rubbed her back until her wails turned into sobs. "I will," he promised. He tried to catch the author's eye, but she wouldn't look at him. "Thank you."

Minutes later he strapped Olivia, who'd managed to calm down, in her car seat ready to go home. He'd find something for Melanie and her parents online. He got into the driver's seat and was about to turn on the ignition when someone knocked on his window. He turned and saw the author wearing a large, dark blue cashmere coat and faux fur hood. He lowered the window.

"Thanks for not saying anything," she said. "I can't let anything ruin this for me." She sent Olivia a cold stare. "Especially her."

"Ruin it for you?"

"She nearly destroyed my life. I admit I'm no angel. I've made mistakes, but that doesn't mean my life has to end, right? My boyfriend dumped me when I got pregnant with her. I already knew he was married with a family of his own, but he didn't have any problem supporting me before. I couldn't believe he turned on me. I lost my place and income and my parents wouldn't let me stay with them because they didn't approve of my lifestyle." She rolled her eyes. "As if they should judge. Mom had more boyfriends than me before she met dad. And at least I had standards. I was living well not hurting anyone.

"But *no*, I was on my own. Living with friends, selling what I could, taking odd jobs. And do you know how bad that was? Do you know what it's like to have some alien creature take over your body and turn it into a walrus?"

Joshua impatiently tapped his fingers on the steering wheel. "I don't think—"

She rolled her eyes again. "Look, maybe some other women like their breasts turned into milk sacks and their stomach stretched like a beach ball, but it was all just ugly to me. I hated every day I was pregnant with her and it was no better when she came." She sent Olivia a look of disgust. "Never stopped crying, sucked my nipples raw—"

Joshua cleared his throat. "Well, I think—"

"And you try traveling cross country with an infant. I pretended to be someone else, just for fun, right? I posted advice and stuff online and people starting paying attention but I wasn't making anything. Then I got a chance to escape. I stood in for a friend at a photo shoot for a local clothing line and I met a guy who overheard me talking to someone about makeup or something. He said he liked my advice and I told him about my blog and he asked me if I had ever thought of being a writer.

"I said hell yes, he said great 'cause he owned a publishing company. He said I could be a brand. And he asked me if I had kids and I knew what he wanted me to say, 'cause he's the kind of guy who's easy to read, like my ex, so I said 'no' and he smiled and said I was perfect. We're an item now and I don't have to worry about where I'm going to stay anymore. I'm older than I look, I can't afford to mess this up. He doesn't even know my real name. Nobody can know about her."

Joshua paused before he said, "What should I tell her?"

"About me?"

He nodded.

"I don't care. Tell her the truth if you want. That her father's a dick and she was the worst thing to happen to me."

No, he'd lie. He was good at that. "Fine nobody will know, but one more thing."

"What?"

"Why me?"

"Why did I choose you at the bus stop?"

He nodded.

She grinned. "I told you I know how to read men. I knew you were one of the good ones."

CHAPTER 42

*M*eeting in the conference room. Ten-thirty.

Joshua stared at the text from Roger.

Important?

Yes.

He sighed and stood. He looked across his desk at his colleague, a man with bushy dark brows and a shock of red hair, who was typing furiously. "Do you know what this meeting is about?"

The man shrugged and continued typing. That didn't bother him. They'd worked well together because neither liked to talk much.

"See you there."

He nodded.

Joshua left his office. It seemed strange he'd been included in any meeting since he soon wouldn't be working there, but if Roger thought it was important for him to be there he wouldn't argue.

He entered the conference room, surprised he was the first one there. He usually wasn't. He took a seat and waited.

When ten thirty-five struck and he was still alone, he texted Roger. **Where is everybody?**

He lifted his head when he heard the door open. Karen walked in looking stylish in a red wool suit with white blouse, which made him think about her dressed in a red robe and wearing Santa hat and telling him he was a bad boy...

She closed the door behind her. "Since you won't return my calls I thought this was the best way to reach you."

He glanced down at his cell phone, before he looked past her at the door. He didn't want to look at her. He didn't want to see Marshall's ring on her finger. He didn't want to pretend that the sight of her still didn't make his heart melt.

"I see."

She walked to the head of the table and took a seat. "There are a few things we need to discuss before you leave."

He nodded.

"But before we begin, I want to make one thing very clear." She typed something on her tablet before she beamed it on the wall.

Joshua took a deep breath before he turned to see what was so important to her. He didn't care what she had to say. How much money she thought they could make. He wasn't staying. He looked at the image and stopped. He didn't see a chart or graph or bullet points. He saw four simple words: **I love you too.**

What?

"Is that clear enough for you?"

He blinked quickly. Was he really seeing this? He turned to her stunned.

She grinned. "I mean it."

"I-I don't understand. You love Marshall."

"Not anymore."

His mind reeled. "But...I saw you kissing him. You kissed him and you didn't stop."

She hung her head ashamed. "I know and I'm sorry. I was—for a moment I wasn't myself. It was what I'd always dreamed. But it was only for a moment." She met his gaze. "It didn't mean anything. Afterwards I only thought of coming home to you and Olivia."

"But my note—"

"Marshall stole it from my lunch bag. I didn't see it. I only discovered the truth by accident. But once I did, I confronted Marshall and he told me everything. It's not the first time he stole something from you. He did something similar twenty years ago."

Joshua frowned. "I don't remember that." He shook his head. "I don't even remember him."

"That's the irony," she said with a sad laugh. "He remembered you and what he did and his guilty conscience got the best of him." She stood and walked towards him. "He won't come between us again."

Joshua rose to his feet not sure if he wanted to run

away or grab her. It hurt to hope. It hurt to let himself believe that she loved him.

Karen studied him, determined to win him back. Her heart race and her knees shook, but she held his gaze. She would block him from leaving if she had to. This time she would fight to make him stay. She'd learned too much about herself these last several weeks. How blind she'd been about Marshall. It embarrassed her. She now understood her mother's words. It wasn't fair to throw away all the love her father had given her for one mistake, no matter how deep the wound. He'd made up for it. She'd held onto a year of hurt and turned it into more than a decade. But no more. The woman who'd kissed Marshall and distrusted her father was gone. She'd learned to forgive herself; she needed Joshua's forgiveness now.

She stopped in front of him. "I made a mistake," she said, holding his fierce gaze, although inside she trembled. "But it wasn't with you. It was not realizing soon enough how much you truly mean to me. I shouldn't have accepted your resignation. I shouldn't have let you go. Will you give me a second chance?"

Joshua took a deep breath and looked away. She couldn't blame him for his hesitation. It had devastated her that he'd seen her weakness. That he'd seen her kissing Marshall. She wouldn't blame him for not trusting her.

"You don't want me to resign?"

She couldn't read his guarded expression. "Of course not. I want you to stay. I'm going to be the new president and we'll—" She stopped when he shook his head. He was turning her down. Dismay crushed her heart. No matter what she said or did she would lose him. He would leave her.

"That won't be enough. I want us to be equals. I want a different kind of partnership."

She grabbed the back of a chair in relief. "Of course. We can—"

His dark eyes met hers, stopping her words in a way no one else could. "I want to be husband and wife." His voice was deceptively calm, like a dark river that hid all its dangers beneath the surface. She held her breath. "Is that a kind of contract you're willing to sign?"

"Absolutely," she said and saw the dark, guarded look leave his gaze, replaced by hope and love. He still loved her. She hadn't lost him.

He gathered her in his arms and wrapped them around her like a warm blanket. "I knew you'd say that," he said before he kissed her and swept away the hurt that had kept them apart.

When he drew away, she laughed. "You knew it, huh?"

"Yes." He gently cupped the side of her face. "But there's something else."

"If you read my note, you know the truth about Olivia."

"I do."

"Just so you know, I'm going to adopt her. We come as a packaged deal."

"You want a wife *and* mother too?"

He nodded.

Karen laughed, her heart bursting with joy. "Well, then that changes everything..."

Five years later...

"Daddy, daddy, tell me the story," Olivia whispered.

Joshua frowned. "The story?"

He and his daughter sat together on the couch in front of the lit Christmas tree. The house still had the scent of the gingerbread cookies they'd baked in the afternoon. It was Christmas Eve and he let her stay up late with him waiting for Santa. She never made it past nine. They'd open presents the next morning before traveling to Karen's parents' house for dinner. He heard Karen's footsteps upstairs as she worked in her office, talking to Marshall who was separated from his wife and estranged from his father. He'd briefly left 3R to fail spectacularly on his own before coming back three years later, begging for any position she could give him. He became an assistant in the marketing department and flourished there.

Joshua glanced at his watch. He'd have to go up and get her soon or she'd work through the night. Their two year old son was already fast asleep.

"Yes, you know," Olivia insisted. "Our Christmas story."

"I don't know our Christmas story," he teased her, knowing very well the story she wanted to hear. The story he told her every Christmas.

She furrowed her brows. "Yes, you do. It's the story about how you found me and how I helped you and Mom love each other and—"

"Since you know the story so well you tell me."

She frowned. "No, I like when you say it. Please."

"All right," he said and she grinned and snuggled up against him with youthful enthusiasm. He loved the feel of her soft, little body next to his. "Once upon a time there was a lonely man..."

She poked him. "You."

He nodded. "Yes, me. And one cold December day, this lonely man found a beautiful baby at a bus stop."

She grinned and pointed to herself. "Me."

He tenderly kissed her on the forehead. "Yes, *you* and the moment the lonely man saw her he knew he'd found his greatest Christmas gift..."

ABOUT THE AUTHOR

Dara Girard, an award-winning, national bestselling author of more than forty novels, from romance to suspense, loves telling stories.

Born in the US to immigrant parents, Dara enjoys pulling from her Jamaican, British, Nigerian heritage and exposure to various cultures to bring what reviewers and fans call "vivid emotional stories" to life. She is best known for her popular Henson Series, the mysterious Clifton Sisters, and the fun Black Stockings Society.

You can write her at:
contactdara@daragirard.com
or
P.O. Box 10345
Silver Spring, MD 20914
If you'd like to receive a reply, please send a self-addressed stamped envelope.

Visit her website to sign up for her newsletter and get sneak peeks, monthly updates on new releases, and special offers.

For more information visit
www.daragirard.com